WARPMANCER
RISE

Book 4 of the Warpmancer Series

Nicholas Woode-Smith

Copyright © 2018

Warpmancer

All rights reserved

This is a work of fiction. Any similarity to real persons, living or dead, is coincidental and not intended by the author.

No part of this publication may be reproduced, stored in a retrieval system, or transmitted in any form or by any means electronic, mechanical, photocopying, recording, or otherwise without the prior written permission of the publisher and the copyright owner.

ISBN: 9781982906894

It is the 36th century of the Old Terran calendar and humanity is spread across the stars.

Zona Nox is dead. Its human defenders and the Xank invaders were caught unaware as the Imperials blighted the planet, rendering it uninhabitable. The survivors of Zona Nox, numbering in the millions, now flock to the ice world of Nova Zarxa, where they hope for safe harbour.

But Nova Zarxa is not safe. The Imperials are still out there, and they never surrender.

Contents

Chapter 1.	Nexus	4
Chapter 2.	Choice	19
Chapter 3.	Agent	34
Chapter 4.	Underworld	44
Chapter 5.	Zeruit	56
Chapter 6.	Reunion	64
Chapter 7.	Knives in the Dark	81
Chapter 8.	Training	86
Chapter 9.	Freedom	97
Chapter 10.	New Struggles	107
Chapter 11.	Anticipation	117
Chapter 12.	Hated	129
Chapter 13.	Governor	139
Chapter 14.	Mutagen	147
Chapter 15.	Fought the Law	157
Chapter 16.	Glossary	180

"Every revolution started as an idea." – Gert the Agitator

Chapter 1. Nexus

Ice became red as the seas of frost reflected the now rising sun. A perpetual snowstorm did little this day to block the star of Extos III as it illuminated the planet, Nova Zarxa. For a planet so often covered in storms, it was an agreeably momentous occasion.

James could not know how auspicious this day was. To him, the light was drearier than on Zona Nox. He could not be expected to know that this was a bright day on planet Nova Zarxa. For, only a day ago, he had never even left Red Sand, the desert of his home planet of Zona Nox - a planet which was now dead. As James and the Troopers had been fighting the Xank, a hidden enemy had infiltrated the planet and eradicated all methods of sustaining life. The Imperials had blighted Zona Nox and James knew that he would make them pay.

'We're approaching Nexus, Grag-Tec starport,' a Marshal Rekkie spoke over the intercom. 'Please prepare for landing.'

Marshal Rekkie was a veteran and war hero whom James greatly respected. It was under a week since they had met, but it seemed like years already. Fighting side by side tended to do that. No bonds were like battle bonds. What started as merely a deal born of necessity had built a relationship between them that would be hard to break. James at least hoped so.

The ship they flew was human in design, but its origin was not. They had flown the Jameson-I Cruiser from a Xank Lectorate ship, the orbiting headquarters of none other than one of the leaders that James had previously sought to defeat. After being captured and shown the truth, his goals had changed. The Word Lector, the head of research and development in the Empire was, in fact, a human exile.

Aven Smith had joined the Xank to seek vengeance against the Imperial Council. Under his new leaders, he had turned a blind eye to the slaughter of his race and even committed his own atrocities. But he had sworn allegiance to James!

James still didn't know what to think of Aven's and the Immortal, Krag-Zot's, pledge of allegiance. The latter had been aiming to kill him only minutes before declaring his undying loyalty. *Some cultures are highly odd*, James noted.

What James did know was that it would be a long while before he could rest easily again. His homeworld was dead and the culprits still lived. By his honour, integrity and, maybe, mostly anger, he would not rest until they were put to justice.

The Jameson-I moved at a much slower pace after entering the atmosphere of Nova Zarxa. Air resistance and adverse weather contributed to a much more sluggish pace as the ship droned towards the docking bay. Even with the icy squalls and potential for turbulence, the ship was still a calmer ride than that of the X-Series ships on Zona Nox. James did not expect that the landing would be harsh enough to warrant buckling himself to the walls or seats of the ship.

Through the light fog and snow, Nexus appeared. While it seemed most of the planet was mere icy tundra, Nexus proved to be a jewel in desolation. A sprawling mass of metallic towers stood ahead of the ship. They rose higher than any tower that was ever constructed in Galis, some of them even rising past the clouds. Connecting the monoliths were a web of connecting tunnels and bridges. Between these were glass domes, revealing idyllic greens within. But James knew that every window and hole was sealed. The air outside was toxic. Beautiful, a shining jewel. Nexus was a diamond in a sea of coal.

The ship began to slow as they approached one of the wider towers. Even now, James could see a thoroughfare of smaller ships passing in and out of a glowing opening on the side of the structure. A gravity beam caught them as Marshal signalled that they wished to land. Their speed slowed to a Mozar's pace as they were pulled in by the docking mechanism. James continued to stare out the window of the Jameson-I, when he felt a hand rest on his shoulder. He turned to see the large broad figure of Ryan.

The ex-gangster stood high above that of James, his shoulders were also broader, framing a set of hard muscle. The brawler was as tough as rocks and James was happy that they were friends. Who could think that he would have come this far with 'Racist Ryan' by his side?

'I used to think I'd never make it here…that I would die back on Zona Nox in some fight with a junkie. That was all I was good for there, anyway,' Ryan sighed. 'Nova Zarxa. In all my life, never thought I'd make it here. Maybe my fate has changed.'

'There is still plenty fighting to do,' James replied.

Ryan seemed to sadden. 'Yes…of course. I'll still die in a fight, just not at home.'

The ship stopped with a sharp jolt as the gravity beam released them onto the platform. Ryan left without a word, heading to the luggage.

Through the door which he disappeared came two non-humans, Quok the Exanoid and Molok the Gray. They were the unlikely members of James' crew. Back on the X51, where James had been forced to choose those who could survive Red Sand after the ship inevitably crashed, he had chosen Quok purely to gain the strength of Molok. Grays were usually weak creatures suitable for labour only due to their discipline and weak will, an odd combination of traits which created a work force which had become more common than that of machinery on the frontier of space. Molok was an oddity for a Gray. He was agile and strong.

Quok was an Exanoid, a race of businessmen and intellectuals. They were not known for their military prowess, besides the uses of their orbital air fighters and army of robotic Syns. He was an odd choice but, either due to sentimentality or an effort to gain Molok's favour, James had chosen to bring the Grag-Tec official along.

Now, as they prepared to disembark the Jameson-I into a Grag-Tec station, James was thankful for his choice.

'Captain James,' Quok called, walking casually towards James with Molok in tow, wearing a toothy grin. 'I wish to thank you for your companionship and choosing us to come on this journey. It has been an enlightening one which will stay with me for quite some time.'

The Exanoid sounded cheerful, and a little carefree. There was no hint of any sign that so many of their allies had died on this escapade and that it had all ended with the death of James' homeworld. Quok was the personification of bliss, when he desired.

Quok nodded his head and continued through the exit of the Jameson-I. To James' surprise, Molok did not follow immediately but instead hung back until Quok was through the doorway. He then walked to James and spoke, an action very unlike him.

'James-Po, I am not one for words, so I will make this quick. As you may have guessed, Quok is very important to me. Like a brother and father. Even though he may seem naïve, he knows very well what is going on. I also wish to extend my thanks to you for allowing him to live. He was not the logical choice back on the X51, but I appreciate it nonetheless. You have earned my respect.'

Molok ended with a bow and left, following his charge.

James was still recovering from the shock of hearing the near-mute speak. He almost didn't notice the survivors of his crew leaving the ship until Marshal came up to him.

Marshal was a man of the elements. He had lived most of his life under the blazing sun and his skin showed it. It was dark and leathery, but the muscle underneath was still useful. Marshal was a strong man and, in some circles, even a hero.

'Are you okay?' he looked concerned.

'As much as I can be,' James attempted a smile. 'Let's go.'

The scene outside the Jameson-I was a sight similar yet not to the Galis starport. Cargo containers rested between ships lodged in deactivated gravity wells. Some ships were being repaired, while others were taking off and landing. Guards overlooked all of this, making sure to keep out troublemakers. It was very much like Galis, but everything was wrong. Instead of rusty, dark metal, there was, instead, light coloured geradite; instead of Troopers, there were

Vacaraptor and Merka guards. This was not Galis, but seemed to rather be a distorted mirror image of James' home.

Ahead of Marshal and James were a cluster of James' allies. Quok and Molok stood to one side, speaking with a well-dressed Gray holding a tablet computer. A little bit further away was Ryan, clutching his Galisian Magnum in his hand and arguing with a Merka guard.

'Skite! What has he got himself into?'

They walked speedily towards the confrontation where they could now hear the source of the argument. Ryan was making a huge scene, speaking loudly and waving his .45 around.

'What the hell do you mean license? I've got rights! I can carry this thing with me wherever I damn well please!'

'Sir, I cannot allow you to continue into the facility with an unlicensed firearm. Governor Dedelux's orders. I will have to confiscate it. Please do not resist,' the Merka guard desperately tried to reason, sweat dripping down his sloped forehead.

Merka were close relatives to the Exanoids. They possessed similar facial features but. instead of a bent spine, they tended to be more hunched, with stouter necks. They were the stronger, more military prone. of the two-races. If Exanoids were pig-men, then Merka were boar-men. Even then, Ryan was taller and more muscle-bound than this guard.

'I will damn well resist!'

Before Ryan could do anything to force the issue, Quok appeared between the two.

'What do we have here? Yurlgaj, what do you have against my apprentice?'

The Merka saluted. 'Welcome back to Nexus, Overseer Quok. I was informing the human of the Trooper Governor's policy on firearms. No unlicensed weapons in the city. Only Troopers and Corporate guards are to carry weapons.'

'Then I see no problem,' Quok smiled, 'Ines Rebeck is my guard, alongside Molok-Po. He carries his firearm by my orders.'

'What about the rest?' the guard indicated Leroy and Grugo, who were both carrying multiple weapons slung over their backs and fronts. 'The other three are Troopers, but these two are civilians.'

'Also guards. You must have heard about what happened on Zona Nox, right? These were my escorts.'

'Ah, then everything is completely fine. Good day, Overseer.' He glanced at Ryan, 'Good day, Ines.'

The Merka walked off in a dignified manner, stopping only to investigate a shipment of meat being carried by a human lady with tattooed arms.

The guard now out of earshot, Quok spoke to the group. 'It has been awhile since I was here on Nexus, so my grasp on local politics is limited. I will try my best to protect all of you, using Grag-Tec's resources if necessary, but I do implore that you exercise extra caution. This isn't Zona Nox and this isn't Galis. Those who fight the law here tend to lose.'

A few of them nodded.

'I will organise accommodation for all of you. If you would follow me…'

James picked up his luggage, a case containing his rifle and supplies, and followed. Quok kept a steady pace, one which would seem brisk for an Exanoid but leisurely for a human. It was not that long before they exited the vast hall of the starport and entered a hallway crafted of geradite and glass.

The hallway was large, allowing space for a crowd or vehicle much larger than James' group. Their footsteps and voices echoed, rising above the sound of the industry in the starport.

A few conversed, but James kept silent. His brooding did not attract social interaction. Quok seemed to be busy talking Marshal's ear off. The veteran appeared interested, but James suspected that that was mere etiquette. Only Ryan seemed genuinely absorbed, as he edged ever closer to the two.

James hung back, an action he noted was particularly uncharacteristic of a leader. A small part of him worried about that, but that feeling was overwhelmed by a pulsating force emanating from beneath him. No one else seemed to notice the almost elemental pull from below, suggesting that only James felt it. It was like a magnet was attempting to tug him downward. Almost unconsciously, he stumbled towards the railing and looked down. A deep blue glow assaulted his vision. Like sunlight, the ground all but blinded him. As his vision adjusted, the light faded and revealed itself to be a sea of crystals.

He felt an energy reaching up from that sea, a familiar grasp of desire and domination. The Warp. Without thought, James put out his hand, grasping at the invisible force. The glass blocked him, but did not abate his instinctual urge to claim that magnificent power. Yet he felt nothing. No power surged into him. It was as if he was drinking from an empty bottle. Desperately, he attempted to siphon the energy. Not an iota passed through the glass.

A hand touched him on the shoulder and he jumped as his trance was broken. Marshal looked at him, visible concern crossing his face.

'What's wrong?'

James clutched his head, the beginnings of a headache starting to emerge. Rubbing his temples, he replied.

'Just feeling a little nauseous. Will be alright in a few.'

'You need to rest. Let's hurry. I don't feel like getting lost in this maze.'

James nodded in agreement and they continued.

The Grag-Tec offices held almost no similarities to those of Galis. While the few office blocks in Galis may have been somewhat stylish in comparison with the rest of the city, they were put to shame by the overwhelming professional luxury of the Grag-Tec facility.

Silver metallic surfaces coated the entire expanse of the Grag-Tec entry hall. Fine green leather upholstery decorated every bit of seating and an extravagant marble fountain dominated the centre. What was the largest difference of them all, however, was the fact that James' crew were the only humans in what seemed the entire complex. They towered over the residents, who ranged from the milky Grays to the bow-legged Exanoids and their stockier Merka cousins. James even spotted some insectoid creatures that he did not recognize.

'Are there any humans in Grag-Tec?' James asked.

'Occasionally,' Quok replied, 'Grag-Tec is meant to be a primarily Gray and Exanoid-run corporation. The treaties after the Glotos III uprising made that a top priority. Grag-Po wanted it that way, so we respect it to this day.'

As they walked through the bustling hall, many stopped to greet Quok and enquire about his journey. He answered in a myriad of languages, even emanating a clicking sound to answer the insect creatures. This multilingualism astounded James, who could only speak colloquial human.

Among the usual smartly dressed Exanoids were the much rarer well-dressed Grays. The aliens were stereotyped system wide as labourers and tribals, so it was not often that they were seen wearing formal clothing. Many carried handheld computers and were hastily typing away, speaking to each other in what seemed to be a mix of Eral'a and native Gray.

As they walked, even more stopped to greet Quok, and even Molok, the latter of whom tended to ignore most advances.

Eventually, they arrived in a circular room. The walls were a white chemical steel called Flensteel. On a planet devoid of metal, Zarxians had to make do with synthetic substitutes. Geradite and Flensteel seemed to be the most popular. The centre of the room was dominated by a large reception desk, manned by a female Exanoid who was busy answering a call on her wireless headset.

Upon spotting the group, the receptionist hung up her call and stood up.

'Overseer Quok, I did not think that you survived the Xank attack. I am glad to see that you are safe.'

She bowed in an odd Exanoid-ish fashion. Quok smiled and replied.

'I wouldn't be here if it was not for James and his companions. They are without accommodation here on Nova Zarxa, so will you do me a favour and find them an apartment?'

'Certainly, Overseer.'

She sat down and began banging some keys on a holographic keyboard

'There are two large apartments available in Residency B-2. Should I call for some attendants to help with luggage?'

'That will not be needed, thank you,' Marshal butted in.

Quok allowed the veteran to make the decision, nodding when the secretary turned to him for approval.

'Here are your key cards,' she smiled a toothy, trained smile. 'I hope you enjoy your stay with Grag-Tec.'

James and Marshal accepted the palm-sized metallic disks. The receptionist stood up once again and bowed.

'Welcome to Nova Zarxa.'

"By the mid-36th century of the Old Terran calendar, humanity had to make a choice. They could forget and prosper, or remember and risk annihilation. It would have been a simple choice, if justice ever was." – Extract from Archivist, Lenda Smitt's, personal memoirs

Chapter 2. Choice

James awoke to the sound of alien pop music and the sight of the artificial sunroof of his apartment. He was sharing the abode with Sgt Yobu and Marshal, while Leroy, Ryan and Grugo stayed in the other apartment. The Grag-Tec residencies were not only for guests and employees, James found out, but also for anyone who could pay rent. Thus, they found themselves neighbouring a quite raucous and newly married Exanoid couple. Their personalities were quite disconcerting as the only ones of their kind on Zona Nox had been quite sedate.

Unable to fall back to sleep, James decided to get out of bed. He pulled himself up and checked the clock on the wall – 32YU. James did not know what in the void it meant. He then checked his own wristwatch – 13:00. It would have been early morning on Zona Nox.

James felt a pang of sadness. It was bound to happen eventually. He had felt so angry over the loss of his home that he had not had any time to mourn.

'No use crying now,' he muttered to himself. So, he fought down the urge to brood and moved towards the bathroom. The room was the usual affair – a shower, basin and toilet. The latter was usable by humans, but like most Exanoid chairs, had a highly crooked back.

James approached the basin and turned on the hot tap. The room temperature in this building was always maintained at a constant rate, but James was used to much hotter climates. The bowl full, James submerged his face. He lifted his head and, with blurry vision, reached out for a towel. He found it and rubbed his face.

As his vision cleared, he froze. In the reflection of the basin mirror, behind him by only a hand-span, was a pale white creature with pointy ears and sharp underbite fangs.

James reacted purely on instinct and swung his arm around, attempting to surprise the beast so he could follow through with a sharp jab to the solar plexus. His arm was caught with ease and he soon found himself hoisted off the ground.

'Your strength is lacking, Boymancer, but I do respect your reflexes.'

It suddenly dawned on him.

'Krag-Zot!'

'Yes, who else would it be?'

James did not answer as Krag-Zot lowered him onto the ground. As he landed, James suddenly realised that he was wearing nothing but boxers. The Areq did not seem to notice or care.

'So,' James panted, 'To what do I owe the pleasure?'

'I am your faithful vassal. What more reason do I need to shadow my liege?'

'Some way of respecting your liege,' James muttered, rubbing the spot where Krag-Zot had gripped him.

'I will not harm you, but I will defend myself when I must. Think of it as a simulation of a proper assassination. A genuine assassin would have killed you by now. Then where would I be?'

James grunted in amusement.

'I'm not a galactic threat. I doubt any assassins are coming after me.'

'On the contrary, Boymancer, you have already begun to make waves in this galaxy. Do not forget that the Lector has pledged himself to you. This is no mere fancy. One of the power brokers of the Empire has sworn to serve what seems to be a simple teenage Trooper. No, you are much more than just that. You have a potential in you; a well of power which could topple societies. In the days to come, you will realise that not only the Warp will serve you, but entire peoples.'

James raised his eyebrow sceptically. 'How do you know this?'

The Areq smiled slightly. 'I have lived for many centuries. You tend to learn a little thing about prophecy in that amount of time. I may be wrong, but I believe the gods' have great plans for you.'

James left the bathroom with Krag-Zot in tow. His section of the apartment was partitioned off from the rest, so James did not have to worry about the others seeing the Immortal. Only Marshal currently knew that Aven and Krag-Zot were allies of James. The rest simply believed that they had managed to escape the Lectorate ship through the virtue of Marshal and James' combat skills.

'Regardless, I will need your help.'

'I am yours to command, my liege.'

James thought for a little bit for questions to ask, but only one came to mind.

'Earlier, I was standing on one of the walkways when I sensed what seemed to be a Warp pull. It seemed to emanate from below.'

'Yes, I know of what you speak. I feel it too.'

'How is that?'

All Warpmancers can feel the pull of Warp. That is what makes us what we are. While others may train themselves to use this art, they will never naturally feel its energy. They aren't like us. The crystals below this city, the same crystals which cover this entire planet are concentrated Warp energy. This must be the first time you have encountered so much, and as a result you are feeling what we refer to as the Hunger.'

James nodded. 'How did so much Warp energy form here? I knew it was an energy mining world, but there must be a reason for the large concentrations here. Warp isn't a natural mineral. It ain't like steel or oil.'

They were now looking outside of the apartment at the crystals below. James felt a slight tug, but was not as lightheaded as the day before. Krag-Zot didn't speak for a long while. James glanced at him every so often. The Immortal's face was blank of emotion.

'This planet – Nova Zarxa you call it – was Resh.'

'Resh? Your homeworld?'

'Was. This was my homeworld, a long time ago. Now…now even the rock itself is different.'

James didn't need clarification. Resh had been blighted by the Imperial Council approximately one-thousand years ago. If Nova Zarxa was Resh, then that meant…

'So, this is what will become of Zona Nox?'

Krag-Zot nodded.

'Then it seems we both lost home worlds to the same enemy,' James said, sadly.

'It seems so, Boymancer. It seems so.'

❖

Krag-Zot had left an hour after his sudden arrival. Well, James presumed that 33YU was an indication of an hour passing. Honestly, he did not know what in Extos was going on. The Immortal had left in an almost impossible fashion as James attempted to seek him out a few seconds later to find him completely gone. His exit was the same as his entry – inexplicable.

Before then they had spoken of many things, but spent equal amounts of time in complete silence, merely staring out at the crystals. They had spoken of philosophy, their home worlds and what James planned to do with his life.

'I don't know,' James had replied, 'I don't know what I'm going to even be doing today.'

'A plan is always needed in life,' Krag-Zot had replied, 'those with a plan for their life always go further than those without. Even if those plans do not come to fruition, it is better to have one than none.'

James still pondered this now. What would he do now? Back on the Lectorate ship he had been consumed by a desire for vengeance, but that fire had now shrunk to a flicker. He still hated the Council, but his rage was not as it once was. James had always been directed in his life. He might have claimed independence and did exercise his autonomy, but he had always had some sort of power to tell him what to do or a goal that needed fulfilling. Even when he was leading his squad across Red Sand, he was being led by the eventual goal of reaching Fort Nox.

What was his goal now?

James' brooding was interrupted by the sound of a stifled yawn as one of the other residents of the apartment woke up. James stood up from the window seat which had been occupying for much of the morning and exited his quarters.

Sgt Yobu stood in the centre of the room, his normally neat military cut hair dishevelled. The Trooper Sergeant stood idly in the middle of the room, his eyes closed with his hand attempting to catch a yawn. James had never seen him more casual. Yobu was usually highly meticulous, loyal and almost robotic in his military stature. This sign of humanity was quite reassuring. Even robots can get tired.

'Good morning, Sergeant,' James called.

The Sergeant opened his eyes wide and quickly turned to salute.

'Sir!'

James waved the formality away. 'We've been fighting side by side for weeks. No need for that. My badge might be larger, but we are equal on the field.'

'Forgive me, Captain, but we are not equal. Your skill far surpasses mine. I do not salute you out of military formality, but out of respect.'

James was truly taken aback, but before he could stutter out a thank you, they were interrupted by Marshal.

'You're up early...'

'Void if I know,' James chuckled, 'I don't know how to tell the damn time here.'

Marshal laughed a genuine laugh. James hadn't heard one for quite some time. It was refreshing.

'Zarxian time is odd. Their day contains 42 human standard hours, but their equivalent to midnight would be 25YU.'

'Very odd,' James concurred, 'but they must think our time eccentric.'

James turned to Yobu, who was a native Zarxian.

'I got used to Zona Nox time quite quickly, but many of my squad mates never got the hang of it,' the Sergeant replied.

James snorted in amusement. 'No wonder it was so easy to bypass patrols. You guys couldn't figure out the time.'

'Pardon?'

'Nothing, nothing.'

In James' favour, his awkward remark was forgotten as they heard a knock on the door. Marshal answered it to reveal the members of James' crew, excluding the aliens.

Ryan stood at the fore, with Grugo and Leroy behind. Six men now stood in the metallic apartment, and James could not help but feel a degree of sadness. The group had once been much larger. For some reason, James felt all the deaths now. He remembered all the men who had died under his command.

'We never had any real time to pay our respects to those who died on Zona Nox,' James explained as his crew members found places to sit around the room. Many of them nodded in agreement. 'Now that we have found some respite, we should remember the fallen.'

James had only given one funeral before. Death was a passing fact in the world, one so common and minuscule that it did not warrant notice. Yet, James felt that his friends deserved remembrance.

'Corporal Tavish,' Sgt Yobu announced, breaking the silence, 'and Private McCallister.'

His head was bowed and his face dry, but James knew that the Sergeant felt pain. He had held it in for so long and continued to do so.

'Briar, Mennis and Porter,' Grugo added. His head, too, was bowed.

More names came: Jherad, Ethran, Dean, Vick and Tim - some of whom James did not know, and some of whom still filled him with guilt.

'May they find happiness and peace - wherever they are.'

The room was left in a tense silence, one which James could not abide. Too much had been left unsaid. Somebody needed to say it. Better it be him.

'I was their Captain, I chose them and they died under my command. Their deaths are mine to bear.'

'James, that is not how anyone should remember them,' Ryan interjected, 'it is unfair to blame their deaths on yourself. For you and for them. They chose to follow you. You did not pull the trigger and you did not order them to the grave. Soldiers die in war. Void, people die all the time. It is demeaning to take away a man's free will by stating that you caused their deaths. Do not let them be remembered as cannon fodder, but as men who died fighting.'

Everyone nodded in agreement. Leroy looked down as he did so. Wet stains were growing on his shirt and pants as tears fell. Each person felt some sort of loss from the past weeks, but with Ryan's speech, James felt a little bit more at peace.

But the meeting was not finished. James had one final thing to say.

'So, here we are.'

Most of the group looked up.

'It's not Fort Nox, but it's something. I was tasked with bringing you to safety and as we have reached the end of our journey. I am saddened, but relieved, to say that this is the end of our journey. The survivors of the X51, few that there may be, are here. We have fought long and hard, but I must say that if I was to do it all over again – I would not choose another group of men. I am proud to have been your Captain.'

There was a period of silence as James concluded. No one uttered a word as they stared at James and then slowly rose as one. All of them stood facing James, rigid and silent. As one, they brought their hands to their foreheads and saluted.

James' eyes moistened, but he didn't cry. His comrades – friends, stood saluting him with all their devotion. Never could he have asked for more.

'A…at ease.'

They ended their salute by bringing their right fist to their heart and then to their side.

'Captain, I will follow you to the grave, if you will let me,' Grugo exclaimed.

This shocked James more than anything else, but before he could reply at all, Ryan spoke.

'I have been given a job with Grag-Tec, but I will continue to help you any way I can, Captain.'

This was followed by Leroy. 'I have never been one for loyalty to anything but a gang, but I will do the same as Ryan. You need help, Cap'n and I will give it.'

Marshal said nothing and only nodded at James. A nod of approval which meant more to James than most.

'Why?' James asked, his voice a hush.

It was Grugo who answered. 'You did more on that Xank ship than just help us survive. There's something special about you and I want to help you do whatever you are planning. Our home's dead. This galaxy let that happen. This galaxy needs change. I want to be a part of it.'

With that, the group said their goodbyes and promised to keep in contact. As James went over to Ryan to shake his hand, the big man only looked at James' petite hand with amusement and instead took him in a big hug.

'You're going to make big changes. I just know it.'

James didn't reply. One by one, everyone left until only Marshal and Yobu were left besides James.

'Well,' Marshal said, as he stood up from his chair, 'I better get going to see my family. Their ship should be docking in a few minutes.'

'Best of luck, we must stay in contact.'

Marshal gave him a knowing look and indicated for him to go off to the side, away from Yobu's hearing.

'Your aura is growing; you've noticed that, haven't you?'

James nodded.

'I would suggest you control it, but I sense some danger approaching. You are going to need followers if Smith is correct. Grugo and Ryan are right; you are going to change something. I don't know what it is, but the fact that you are one of the first human Warpmancers in centuries is proof of that already.'

Marshal left after that, leaving only Yobu to stand silently with James in the now almost empty apartment. Even the alien pop music next door had stopped.

The sergeant placed a hand on James' shoulder.

'It's time to go meet up with the fleet.'

"Corporations are to companies what stars are to planets. Companies practice their business on a planet, while corporations span entire systems. It is highly common to find planets totally under the control of a single corporation." – Extract from "Wealth of the Galaxy" by Jherin Kura'kaia

Chapter 3. <u>Agent</u>

Lying before Danny Marzio was a white blotch in a sea of black. The gigantic snowball was the legendary Nova Zarxa – a planet jointly owned by the human Troopers and the alien corporation, Grag-Tec. Even as an isolationist mob boss, Danny could not help but learn a lot about the corporate world. Its only real reason for existing was crystal mining, which Grag-Tec owned the sole monopoly over. In exchange for security, they allowed the Troopers to maintain a base and city on the planet. The air was toxic, and the temperature was too cold for comfortable living. Terraforming was out of the question, however, as it would eliminate the crystals that were the lifeblood of Nova Zarxa's economy.

Instead of living on the surface, which was covered with icy crystals, the entire population inhabited skyways and large skyscrapers. The capital, Nexus, was basically a huge plat-formed city on stilts, somewhat reminiscent of Titan City.

Past that, Danny knew very little about the internal struggles of Nova Zarxa. It had never been his business or desire to have anything to do with the planet.

'Oh, how things change,' Danny muttered as he gazed out the space station window. Occasionally, a smaller ship would race past the window. Some bore the Aegis symbol – a red globe representing Mars – while others bore other symbols as they sped straight towards the planet. Many more just floated idly around in orbit. Ships like these were what Rob had grown up in.

Danny felt a tinge of sadness at that thought and soon fought it down. He knew he would have to get over it. He was supposed to be a sociopathic criminal and killer – not one to cry over the deaths of annoying kids. Yet he could not help but feel melancholic. Rob didn't deserve to die. Many of Danny's previous henchmen also didn't deserve to die, but for some reason Rob's death continued to stick with him. Maybe it was that he was just a boy. A good boy living in a bad world. Maybe it was a change in Danny himself. All he knew was that he could not get the death of Rob Starkin out of his head.

Ships of all shapes and sizes continued to fly past Danny's viewing window, a special compartment of his residence on the Aegis capital ship – the Athena.

The Athena was a custom Olympian Class Hive Ship. It had been constructed in the skydocks of Mars and was the pride and joy of the corporate fleet construction industry. It was a monolithic starship, capable of warp travel between systems without the need to find an appropriate gravity well. It was a gravity well.

The ship was the HQ and base of operations of the head administration of the Aegis Corporation. Contrary to popular belief that Aegis' intelligence operations were directed from Mars, the Athena played host to the true workings of Aegis. Thousands of Aegis employees, soldiers, mercenaries, syns and officials lived on the ship. Housing and amenities were provided in the residency wing while two hangars were stationed in each wing. There were four outer wings with one main pillar. These being residency, Intel, military and agricultural. The pillar hosted the central command.

Danny sighed. The enormity of the structure often left him speechless. The ship itself seemed to be larger than some districts of Galis.

Galis – now that was another thing that was dead. Never would Danny ever see his home and empire again. It was gone, forever.

Danny's silent pondering was interrupted by the mechanical sliding of the door behind him. He turned to see a familiar face. The lady who stood in the doorway was curvaceous, yet muscular. She was tall and broad of shoulder. There was power in this woman. A sense of presence. She looked to be middle aged, but even in his youth, Danny doubted that he could take her in a fight. Fair or not.

Big Momma was the current top agent of the Aegis intelligence corps. She was charismatic, friendly, cheerful and ruthless. Many things were uncertain in this world, but Danny knew that if one thing was certain – it was that messing with Big Momma seldom worked out in your favour.

'Don, you've been sulking up here for hours. You may not be up for it, but you must goddamn pretend that you are. You are an Aegis agent now. That means faking enthusiasm.'

Don it was a title Danny had held back in Galis. Don Marzio – boss of the largest racketeering organization in Red Sand. That was no mean feat. Before the Xank invasion and Imperial blighting, Danny had been at the top of the food chain. Trooper governors ate out of his hand.

Now, he was merely an agent-in-training. Well, it was a start.

'Just watching the traffic,' Danny forced a grin, 'who could think there could be traffic jams in space? I know that the Athena sure ain't helping.'

Big Momma smiled, but Danny knew that she had seen through the cheap ruse.

'Traffic jam or not, you need to make an appearance to at least this dinner. You're leaving this evening. It would be impolite to just leave your cousin and friends without saying proper goodbyes,'

Danny shook his head for no real reason. 'I know, Big Momma, I know.'

He paused and spoke again. 'It's kinda unreal, isn't it?'

'What is?'

'Space. Well, us in space. Who could think that above the ground, our ground, there is a landless world of nothingness yet containing so much? Who could think that we could get there, travel there and live there. Sure, scientists have answers, but I'm no scholar. I only ask, how do we control nothingness?'

Big Momma shrugged. 'Void if I know. I've been space faring since I was a girl. Living on one planet for your entire life, that is what I can't understand. Regardless, you are trying to distract me and I will have none of that. Come to dinner.'

'Yes, yes I should go.'

Big Momma left and Danny soon followed, but not before staring one last time on the icy globe of Nova Zarxa. A planet which he had been commanded, only a day before, to conquer.

❖

Boris had moisture in his eyes, even if he wouldn't admit it. He took Danny in a hug reminiscent of a Mozar stampede.

'We must stay in contact this time. Not like in Red Sand. You will call, right?'

'There's no Teeth of Storms to stop me this time. We'll talk.' Danny said it, but he didn't mean it. He liked his cousin, but maintaining relations was just not in his nature. He would talk, but it would have to be Boris' move. That was just who Danny was. He did not mind relationships, just the act of maintaining them.

After finally being released from the crushing vise grip of Boris' seemingly titanium arms, Danny moved onto the next one of his companions.

Krena was not someone he knew well, as much as he wanted to. If he was to have a type, it would probably be Krena. The Don was used to a sea of floozies and pretty dames literally paid to like him. Krena, on the other hand, was independent, tough and gorgeous. She was a dark blonde with shoulder length hair. Her skin was pale, showing her southern hemisphere heritage. Danny had never seen her with less than her cult armour on, but predicted that her body was both supple and well-muscled.

Danny gave her a long and intense look – even if a bit creepy – before giving her a nod of respect. She nodded back. Then he moved onto the last of his companions.

Viper, even if pale, seemed a dark figure. He stood taller than Danny and in contrast to Danny's tanned skin, looked to have the complexion of snow. His eyes were slanted and his dark hair was kept gelled into spikes. Viper was the quiet sniper and assassin of what once was the Grooks. A small, yet respected gang run by Boris. He was a man of few words, but strong principles. Danny had previously thought him sociopathic, but now thought differently. Viper was a decent killer, but he had integrity and an intense loyalty to both his friends and ideals. Danny was proud to call him friend.

They both shared a nod of understanding before Danny moved off. They had all been standing in a welcoming area outside the departure zone of the small hangar. Danny knew that before he left, he would have one final person to meet.

Ignoring Boris' quite inappropriate weeping, Danny advanced through the wide metal frame towards the departure zone. He heard a metal thunk as the gate shut. There was no sound after that but that of his breathing. It struck Danny now that it may very well be a very long time before he saw his companions again. He was feeling a tad bit of regret.

At the end of the tunnel of silence, Danny came to another mechanical doorway. This one was labelled 'Departures' in large red lettering. It opened automatically to reveal a large hangar area. Side by side, beside a small spaceship of which design Danny did not know, was the CEO of Aegis and his agent, Big Momma.

Now that Danny thought about it, Quentin Wivern was now his boss. It felt somewhat odd having someone giving you orders. Even back in Titan City, while a member of Boris' gang, Danny had still held a position of authority and influence over his cousin. He didn't feel that he would be able to extend the same effect over the CEO of one of the largest human owned corporations in the galaxy. Quentin was a tall, gangly fellow with dark hair and a dark complexion. He seemed to be well-tanned but Danny doubted that it was from labouring in the outdoors. Technology did exist which could replicate a natural tan. Danny's complexion was much more genuine.

The CEO grinned as he approached. Usually boisterous, it was odd to see Big Momma to his side looking sullen.

'Agent Marzio, I must say again how glad I am to have you on the team. Big Momma here is the best in human space, but she can't be everywhere at once.'

'It's an honour, Mr Wivern. I have my orders and will report back in the discussed manner.'

Quentin nodded and then indicated for Danny to enter the shuttle.

'This pod will take you to the public starport. It is preprogramed, so don't worry about flying it.'

He fiddled with a few buttons and the door to the shuttle opened. Danny entered, but before the door closed, was stopped by the CEO, who was still smiling, good-naturedly.

'I should not have to mention what will happen to you if you betray us – right, Don?'

Danny nodded.

'Good, good. I trust you will be able to independently solve this little issue of ours quickly. Farewell.'

After the door to the shuttle closed with a metallic clang and click, Danny could not help but snort in bemusement. This was anything but a little issue.

"Shadows are everywhere. So, if one wants to see everything, hear everything, and know everything – they must become a shadow." – Rev Deakas, Spymaster of the Trooper Order, 3540

Chapter 4. <u>Underworld</u>

The trip to the surface was quick and quiet. The pod sailed smoothly through the air once past the atmosphere. Even the landing was calm as the pod was caught by an electromagnetic arm. The starport in Galis never had something like that. Upon exiting the pod, Danny realised that the hive which was the Nexus starport was anything but Galis. When the Galisian starport was more akin to a scrapyard with landing pads, this was more like an insect hive. Ships ranging from small to gargantuan came whizzing through every second, making Danny dizzy and disorientated.

Danny shook himself from his daze and turned towards the exit. Aegis had setup all the necessary paperwork he would need to get through security with ease. As he approached the security guard, a Trooper with a black shield badge signifying his role, a flash of his paperwork let him pass. He was in.

Danny became more and more convinced that Nexus was an insect hive. Holes dotted hundreds of buildings, and that was only what he could see from the window. According to his locator device, he was currently in an area called a transit – a building given the sole purpose of a hallway.

He knew where he would have to go and he was looking forward to it. Darkness was an element Danny was familiar with and he knew that this part of his mission would be relaxed, if not enjoyable. So, Danny searched his locator and then selected his destination. He set off for the slums.

❖

Finding the slums had been harder than Danny had previously thought. Unlike Titan and Galis, there were no overt shacks or tenements to mark the residences of the poor but rather a change in business practices. Due to the dangers of the outside environment, buildings on Nova Zarxa were subject to strict regulations. As such, even the poorest area still looked somewhat luxurious and sophisticated.

The area which Danny now stood was like every area within this silver shimmering hive. Both floor and walls shone metallic silver and bright white lights trailed along the roof. Danny was sure that this area was the slums, however. His first clue was the lack of any visible Trooper patrols or any corporate presence. His second was the fact that he was propositioned by several prostitutes at least three times upon entering the structure.

The geradite which was used to construct most of the buildings across Nexus did not rust or need painting, so there were very few signs of degradation. Instead, Danny had to look at the actions of the people. Mostly humans lived in this area, but Danny did see quite a few Grays. What both races had in common were that they looked on edge. This was not an area to feel safe. If Big Momma's debriefing was anything to go by, Danny would also feel quite unsafe if he was not allowed to carry a gun. Luckily, Aegis did carry enough influence to give him permission to carry a sidearm. He was still not allowed to show it.

'What type of society bans owning guns?' Danny had said to Big Momma, 'do they want everything to descend into chaos?'

Big Momma had just laughed and replied, 'I agree with you, but many don't. That license will let you through most guard points, but don't go around waving the thing.'

Danny stood at the edge of the starting line. He could say that his mission had started upon receiving it on the Athena, but had not actually accomplished anything yet. Now he was going to attempt the first milestone of his task.

To his left, he noticed an almost familiar sight. Flanked by a heavyset man wearing a tight leather jacket and a much thinner man smoking a cigarette was a red neon sign which read: Club Phoenix.

If there ever was a place to find information, it was a tavern and from the sounds of raucous merry making, this was such an establishment.

The bouncer with the leather jacket only gave him a sideways glance as Danny entered. Aegis had made sure to outfit him in the common fashion of the city so to avoid suspicion and it seemed that it worked. Only his olive skin drew any sorts of looks.

The tavern was a lot more spacious than what it seemed on the outside. It was partitioned into various sections, with two central areas - a bar and a dance platform; very different from Galis. What was the most different, however, was the blaring music. It had no lyrics or contained any instruments that Danny recognized.

Danny could not help but cover his ears as he approached the bar. He had to wade through a veritable sea of dancers who had no concept of personal space. One guy bumped into him and saw him covering his ears.

'You don't like Squogg Punktron?' the dancer shouted over the music, still doing an odd dance as he nodded his head up and down and waved his arms.

Danny shook his head.

'Try the lounge,' he shouted again, pointing towards a doorway at the end of the hall.

Danny nodded in gratitude and waded through the ocean of cacophony.

Upon exiting the crowd and entering the lounge, Danny could not help but feel a profound sense of relief by the fact that no music permeated through the seemingly open doorway. Only the quiet chatter of people in a variety of seats could be heard. Much more pleasant compared to 'Squogg Punktron'.

A bar took up the centre of the room and that is where Danny went first. He had a mission to accomplish and the sooner he started, the sooner he could get it done.

Taking a seat at the bar, he ordered the first thing the bartender offered – a luminescent blue drink - and then waited. Danny had always been a reasonable judge of character and it was not long until a man bearing the desired character took a seat next to him. The man wore a yellow jacket with pads on the front and shoulders. He kept a thin goatee and short spiky hair. What interested Danny the most, however, was that he had slanted eyes like Viper.

'There are two gangs of interest in Nexus,' Big Momma had said, 'the Ganru and Berrin. The former will be the easiest to recognize. Viper's kin are a rare breed and it is even rarer to find one this far from Sekai who is not a member of the Ganru.'

The man took a seat and Danny waited a little bit before turning to him and introducing himself.

'Howdy, partner.'

'What?' the man immediately replied, a look of unenthusiastic bafflement on his face.

Danny inwardly swore at himself and tried again.

'Mick Spinner,' he put his hand before him to shake. He received none in return.

'My name is none of your damn business, black-shirt. Shove off!'

'Is that anyway to greet the man who is going to pay for your drink?'

Like magic, the man's expression changed and he shook Danny's hand.

'Tenigawa Ruma.'

'Well, Mr Ruma…'

'No, Ruma is my first name, Tenigawa is my surname.'

Well then you should have said that in the first place, Danny wanted to say. Instead he smiled.

'Of course; so, Mr Tenigawa, I find myself in this establishment and city with honestly very little knowledge of how I could make a living. Captain of my crew went broke and dumped us all here, you see. Anything you'd suggest I do?'

Tenigawa took a sip from his drink and then answered. 'What sort of ship you on? What you do on it?'

'You could call it a merchant vessel, of sorts. I…well, I was a specialist in let's just say acquiring goods and information.'

Tenigawa immediately turned away from Danny. 'No jobs for you. Corporate monopoly. Sorry, I better be going.'

Danny inwardly swore but feigned a polite nod. The man was obviously skittish – not something Danny was used to from a gangster. Well, Zona Nox had been a planet run by gangs.

A fluke, Danny wanted to think, but the way the patrons stared at him made him doubt that. Something was going on; something which put fear into murderers and thieves alike.

❖

Danny had visited around five taverns, supposedly called clubs, before the waning of the sun. While the built-up areas lacked natural light, the walkways connecting them were mostly glass.

His luck in each club was the same every time. Either he spotted no one of interest, or whoever he tried to converse with snubbed him and disappeared.

From these many transits, Danny could look out onto the tundra and down onto the crystals which gave Nova Zarxa its wealth. From here, he was also capable of telling the approximate time (as the public clocks sure didn't help). It was probably the tenth time he had crossed a walkway like this today and he could not help but notice the dark cloudy skies grow ever darker. Night had arrived and Danny could feel his weariness catching up with him.

Finding accommodation was easy. Entire skyscrapers were devoted to hotels and rentable apartments, after all. Danny had a high budget, but he did not want to draw too much attention. He would search for modest accommodation, and thus he went to the modest hotel district.

As he walked through the 'Blue Guest District' he noticed as the lights on the walls and ceilings began to wane.

A computer or admin team must oversee controlling internal lighting, Danny mused, *keeps away the fever.*

Many of the doorways that he passed possessed a screen with the same words, 'Apologies, we are booked out. Sorry for the inconvenience,' in a multitude of languages.

Danny had not dwelled on it earlier, but now the fact that Nova Zarxa was playing home to a tide of refugees truly struck. He passed a line of stalls selling goods with one customer arguing with the merchant.

'What in the void is this?'

'Credits, it's credits…'

The man held a hand full of green notes – Galisian notes.

'I've been a merchant my whole life and have never seen this. Go scam someone else, counterfeiter!'

The man from Galis retreated like a beaten dog, bumping into Danny and apologizing hastily. As he collided, the man looked up.

As his third or fourth 'Sorry' left his lips, he recognized Danny's face.

'Do...Don Marzio? Is that you?'

Danny winced, he had not accounted for this. 'You must have me mistaken with someone else.'

The Galisian looked away, disappointment almost palpable. 'Oh, you look quite like him.'

He began walking away. 'He might've been a criminal, but he did us good. We had something then in Galis, now I have nothing…'

Danny stopped him before he could get any further. He shoved 500 credits worth of Aegis bonds into his hand and then beat a hasty retreat.

Danny could not see the man's expression, but he knew that he had a tear in his eye.

❖

It was around half an hour later (by Danny's estimation, as the clocks were insane) when he found a hotel with vacancies. He booked a single bedroom at the back. It was a bit too expensive for his liking, but a bed was a bed.

'You're lucky you got here in time. I only have one room left,' the owner had said. Danny grunted in reply, handing her some corporate bonds as payment.

Alone in the small room, he examined it. If anything, it was clean – if a bit lifeless. The only sense of visual warmth was the presence of three portable data tablets under the end table. Danny personally preferred books crafted of paper, but he understood the expense. He had seen a few people reading earlier in the day, but they all seemed to possess some sort of odd portable computer. Upon questioning a merchant (and receiving some odd looks) he learned that Nexus possessed a network which allowed owners of these tablets to download virtual books.

Due to the Teeth of Storms, wireless networks couldn't achieve the possible stability to function, so such technology became useless on Zona Nox. Instead they relied on paper-books and data tablets – disposable computers possessing single books.

One book – A Melancholy of an Extinct Race – caught Danny's eye and he began reading.

❖

Danny did not remember when he fell asleep, nor did he remember waking up. All he knew now was that he was not in the hotel anymore.

It was dark – painfully so. Blackness surrounded him to the extent that he could not even perceive his own body. He felt like a floating brain in a sea of nothingness. Even his breathing was silent, with the only sound to fill the void being a low buzz emanating from outside the blackness.

Danny could not know for sure, but a small part of him smiled. It seemed he had contacted the gangs.

"Upon militarizing the Zangorian race, the Xank needed a method in which to control reproduction while avoiding petty irritations such as maternal bonds. Thus, every male Zangorian's seed was taken and stored – awaiting synthetic fertilization of eggs lost by their mothers." – Aven Smith, "My Time with the Xank"

Chapter 5. <u>Zeruit</u>

The air was hot yet wet. Leri had never felt it, but it somehow felt as if he had been born into it. Of course, he now knew that to be a lie – but his heart still felt that Zeruit was his home. His false memories were still strong, even if he was aware of them being fake. Fake was an incorrect term, however. Leri's memories were real. They were records of real events. They were more accurate than any other synthetic record or historical re-imagining. For Leri held the remembrance of his people within his head. A history spanning hundreds of years. It was a burden and treasure that he had yet to come to terms with. It would be awhile before he had the chance.

Back on the flagship of the Word Lectorate, Leri had come to many realisations. He had realised that he was not who he thought he was, he had realised that his memories were ages old; he had realised that none of this mattered. All that Leri cared about now was vengeance. Vengeance for his people brought by cold hard metal and simple heroism.

He took a Word Lectorate's transport ship to Zeruit. He had not paid attention to time on his journey. His only indication of the duration of the trip was the amount of food he had consumed. He was alone, except for a silent Krugar pilot. They never spoke and that suited Leri just fine. Each of them had separate supplies and separate parts of the ship. In fact, Leri never ventured far out enough to speak with the Krugar. He instead remained in his quarters – studying the notes that the Lector had given him on Zeruit.

Some of the information was what he expected – details on the geography of facilities and fortresses – while others filled him with revulsion. Atrocities such as the breeding programmes, ethnic cleansing and gender separation. While reading, Leri could not help but feel a familiar rage boil up inside. He calmed it, knowing that now was not the time. He had to wait. Wait, plan and grow. Only after that could he consume Zeruit in his fires of revolution.

But that space journey was over now.

Now he stood at the brink of a dark crevice in the hillside. The ship he had been travelling in seemed to have been a stealth vessel, as it managed to bypass all security and land on the surface of Zeruit.

Behind him was a jungle. Leri's only living memory of such a thing was on his campaign on Grengen. He had been a part of the body-budget then. Those jungles filled him with dread, but these colourful leaves and plants did not do the same to him. Rather, they empowered him. The sweet smell of fruit, and cleansing moisture in the year. This was home.

Ahead of him was a cave as dark as void. He could not see inside. He entered.

Leri's journey was one of complete darkness for what seemed like hours. The only sound was that of his footsteps and breathing. A symphony of clacking and hushing. It was enough to drive lesser men insane. Leri was no lesser man.

Then, eventually, he saw light. It was a meagre thing. Only a small candle in the darkness. Yet, it was something. Light in darkness was hope. As small as it was, Leri could not help but feel a sense of anticipation.

'Kurag Leri nuro Zeruit, I presume.'

A voice sounded from the blackness.

'I do not speak with shadows,' Leri spoke loudly, 'reveal yourself and I will answer.'

The faint light grew until it managed to illuminate the centre of the room, revealing a table and chair. Sitting upon the chair was an insect-like creature standing as high as a Zangorian. A Gleran.

'I see you, Kurag. It seems that the Lector was right to send you. You are well-spoken…for a Zangorian.'

'It seems I'm not a normal Zangorian – and you not a normal Gleran. How do you speak to me?'

Through the six eyes and twin mandibles, it was hard to tell, but Leri somehow recognized a grin of sorts.

'Like you, I am a freak of my people. Physically, I am the same – yet mentally I hold something that my people do not; cannot. Sentience. Free will.'

There was a pause as the Gleran stood and offered his hand in a form of greeting unfamiliar to Leri.

'I am a freak among my people, like you. Yet unlike you, I am one of a kind. I am a genetic mutation seen as an atrocity within my species. I am a Gleran of the Vulzthan

Hivemind yet I am not. While my kin do not think, feel or understand without the all-consuming control of the hivemind, I can function independently. I am a sentient, like you, yet that is what makes me a freak. I am Peron the Thinker and I have been tasked with helping you free this world.'

Leri took the Gleran's hand as he presumed that was the purpose of the greeting. The Gleran shook it and let go.

'Are you ready, Kurag? These are not my people, yet I feel an overwhelming urge to free them. My people cannot be freed, so better that I use my brain to help free those that can.'

Leri did not reply. Instead he gazed upon the table top. Items dotted the surface. A blaster, a wrist-blade and…an arm. All were translucent and flickering.

'We can never be ready, Gleran. We are merely given our lot, throw the dice and wait for better numbers. I'm going to keep rolling. Give me the dice.'

'Good, good,' Peron whispered, 'It seems that Smith chose wisely.'

The Gleran indicated for Leri to follow him as he walked into the darkness. Leri followed as the light around the table disappeared, replaced by a single beam illuminating Peron as he walked.

'I see that you have sustained an injury. It is not often that those of your race can live with such a wound. As such, the Lector requested that I source for you…a treatment. You are going to need many tools in this war you are about to start. Wit, brawn and a sharp tongue. Most of all, two hands.'

Leri rubbed the stump of his arm, memories of a fight with a human with a streak of silver hair coming back to him. It was one of his more recent and genuine memories.

'Do not despair. The Lector has connections far beyond what the Xank recognize. He has arranged for a replacement arm. Trust me; you will prefer the new one much more than the old.'

Leri could not help but be blinded as a white light burst to life, lighting up the entire room.

After his eyes had adjusted, Leri examined the room.

The walls were crafted of smooth silvery-white metal. They gave no reflection and emitted coldness. Above everything, the room seemed clean – a medical bay.

Dominating the centre of the room was a contraption the likes of which Leri had never seen before. Computers and blinking lights were connected to pistons and engines, which were further connected to a multitude of different sized mechanical arms.

'This,' Peron announced, 'will remake you. Do not mourn the loss of your limb. Everything that can be lost can be regained. You will come to never miss your old arm again. This new arm will be a symbol. It will be your salvation. Your hope. Your rebirth. Your revolution…'

❖

It still stung, even hours after the surgery had finished. It was a pain that Leri could tolerate. Especially now that he held his new mechanical arm out in front of him. Crafted of titanium and metals that Leri had never even heard of, the arm was a beauty to behold. It shone in the light and possessed talons which even the Infiltrators would envy. It was capable of things no normal organic arm could ever do and allowed for the extension of weaponry which connected directly to his neuro-function. It was a weapon built for not just a revolutionary – but an emperor.

As he experimented with his new limb, he trudged along the path that Peron had indicated to him.

The path led to the first destination in his campaign - an agricultural facility with a record for disobedience. It was a rebel base as far as the Xank went, but a slave camp as far as Leri wanted it to be.

The settlement was a male area with non-warrior Zangorians working the worm farms. After one too many strikes, the Xank had sent in a robotic guard force to keep the workers in line.

Leri knew that that would change. Robots and drones may guard it now from uprising, but Leri was no usual rebel. He was a veteran of the Word Lectorate. His sector created robots – he would just as easily destroy them.

As Leri hiked the dark tunnels to the settlement, he noted the name of the settlement.

Bexong – the city where a revolution would begin. The birthplace of the death of an empire.

"Troopers are for justice? Then why do we sit and allow the greatest crime in our history go unpunished? The High Council are cowards. Your generals are cowards. The Troopers are cowards!" – Aven Smith to Marshal before his disappearance

Chapter 6. Reunion

There was no joy as the survivors of Zona Nox exited the ships which had carried them from the jaws of death. There were no cheers, no singing, no unnecessary speaking or even any sense of relief. People had lost homes, livelihoods, families and their planet. Troopers had failed in their duty. Nathan knew that there was nothing to celebrate.

The Imperial Council had made their move. A small part of him knew that he should have been more terrified. Instead, he felt only numb. He had felt too much pain. His scars were only a small reflection of what he felt. Overcome with despair, he now felt only void. There was no point feeling anymore, if this was all that he could feel.

Nathan shuffled along with the rest of the Troopers aboard the carrier. His recovery had been quick, even if the lasting effects would last his lifetime. He was expected to march like the rest. He didn't mind. His place was with his squad, what was left of it. To be honest, there was no squad anymore; just a ragtag group of survivors from a myriad of units that Nathan had been acquainted. There was no Galis City Trooper Patrol, there was no Fort Nox Engineering Corp; there was no Fort Nox. But there was the Troopers. It would take a lot before that was taken away. Yet, Nathan feared just that. The Imperial Council was a nightmare. Of all the powers in the galaxy, only they stopped the Troopers. No corporation, rebellion, warrior race or alliance had shaken the Troopers before – the Imperial Council would change that.

Nathan had no fortress now. His purpose, his unshakeable family, was in jeopardy.

He instinctively filled in the forms to pass the barrier. The processes were different here than on Zona Nox. Technology was better. Due to the Teeth of Storms, administration and communication on the planet surface had been hard, if not impossible. On Nova Zarxa, computers and a wireless network of servers replaced pen, paper and filing cabinets. Nathan was only to type in his name and squad. The computer figured everything else out.

Bustling along, Nathan's mind could not help but shift back to the trip after the fall of Zona Nox. What many had first believed to be an invasion had been much worse. The once red and white planet was now consumed by black clouds. It was a dead world and even if very few of the Troopers realised the significance of the darkness, they all knew that there was no home to go back to. They had failed.

Noise grew as the regiments marched through the silvery halls of the Trooper spaceport. They kept to a tight formation as only a military unit could. To either side of the walkway were even more landing zones, with even more ships releasing a horde of Troopers and refugees alike.

Troopers were immediately sent to the line where they were ordered to march towards the rallying point for re-assignment. Refugees were bustled off by Zarxian Troopers wearing yellow armbands. *Military police*, Nathan guessed.

Trooper worlds seldom had military police, rather relying on de-centralization of leadership to fight corruption and misconduct. Nova Zarxa was different, however, as it possessed a single governor.

The refugees seemed frightened and the police did not seem to care. A group of refugees were shoved and Nathan felt a tinge of guilt rising from the fact that he could not help them. Even if standing and healthy, he was still just as helpless as when he was stuck in the hospital beds. Even if only scarred rather than bleeding out, he was still unable to change a thing.

They passed squads of military police talking with officers of the Zona Nox Troopers. Even if lower ranking, the policemen seemed to hold an air of arrogance and superiority. They spoke down to the Captains, lieutenants and sergeants that they met, even though they were only privates and corporals. This was not the Trooper way.

Pasted upon the walls and airing on screens were posters and broadcasts with the image of a man wearing the garb of a Council General – Governor Dedelux. Dedelux was not a Council General, but his uniform was evidence enough that he thought of himself as one. Each poster held a message – "Loyalty is safety. Dedication delivers victory."

Nathan shook his head. This was not the Trooper way.

The march ended as they entered a large hall with a glass roof. The plaza was around the size of the courtyard at Fort Nox, but a glance downward would reveal cracks and lines. The room was makeshift. Every wall could be moved or taken down to create a temporary expanse. Otherwise, it was a normal complex.

Nexus was large, but not nearly as colossal as Fort Nox or even nearly as expansive as Galis. They had to make do with technology to reduce the need for land.

Without the need for formation, Troopers next to and behind Nathan began to spread out and search for comrades from the other ships.

Nathan did not move except to allow others past him. He was a single speck in a sea of red and black waves. As he gazed upon those surrounding him, he saw a myriad of relief as well as despair. Like before, he felt nothing.

Nothing until he saw a familiar face appear through a doorway.

❖

James and Yobu had been faced with suspicion when they had informed the Troopers with yellow armbands that they were survivors of Zona Nox. Only recognition of Yobu's Zarxian ID and his insistence that James was a fellow Trooper allowed them entry into the Trooper Headquarters.

Upon entry, they were the subject of a range of harsh looks from masked Troopers. Every single one of them possessed a yellow armband – something James had never seen on a Trooper before.

'They're Dedelux's force,' Yobu had said, 'they answer to him first.'

'Dedelux?'

'The Trooper Governor here on Nova Zarxa. He is more controlling than the governors you had in Galis, so be careful. This is no haven for criminals. This is Nova Zarxa, where freedom is a privilege.'

The stares of Dedelux's Troopers kept them quiet for the rest of the walk, all until they exited the confined tunnel into a huge hall filled with Troopers without their masks. Even if packed to the brim, many of the Troopers within seemed lost. Many were embracing comrades but even more were hastily looking for a friend who was not there.

But that was not what James was staring at, for he had spotted a face he recognised.

Everything seemed to go silent. Only the beat of James' heart echoed in his eardrums. When Yobu left his side to meet with his friends, he did not notice. All he saw was the Trooper with the silver streak in his hair and how he saw him.

Slowly, he advanced into the crowd. Somehow, many made way for him. The Trooper also made his way towards James, but his way was blocked and his going, slow.

But eventually, they stood face to face.

'James?' the Trooper asked.

'Yes,' James replied, simply.

Nathan smiled.

❖

All the numbness and pain of the past while seemed to evaporate at once as Nathan stared at James. The trainee he had saved and recruited in Galis all those months ago was still alive and he had never felt so much relief in his life.

As they stared at each other, Troopers began to notice and realise that James was the very same Trooper who had been seen in broadcasts back on Zona Nox.

'What happened to you?' James suddenly asked, concern showing openly in a frown.

'Me? Oh!' Nathan realised that James was referring to the now white scars crossing his face.

'During the siege, I entered a melee with a Zangorian commander. I destroyed his arm so he attempted to destroy my face. I won, but not without wounds. But enough of that – I haven't seen you…since the Outpost in Red Sand. What have you been doing? How did you get that?' Nathan asked, pointing at the insignia signifying James as a Captain and Strike leader.

'A long, long story…'

'Well, we want to hear it,' a Trooper piped in.

James immediately gazed around and found that they were completely circled by a group of black and red clad Troopers. All of them were from Zona Nox.

'I saw you on the net-screen back in the fort! How did you take down that craft?' another Trooper asked.

'Were you the one who found the tank?'

'Did you really meet Marshal Rekkie?'

'How did you get off the planet?'

Question after question came flying at James. He couldn't catch enough time to answer a single one, until he heard one different from the rest.

'What happened down there? Why's the sky black?'

'Don't be stupid, Mahone. He don't know that.'

James' stare seemed to silence every Trooper in the circle. Nathan also felt it. A pang of coldness biting up his neck, drawing his attention to James.

'I know what happened there,' James said quietly, yet somehow loudly as the rest of the room seemed to turn towards him.

'Xank?' a Trooper shouted.

'No, the Xank were merely a distraction. They always have been,' James replied.

'We know that the Imperials were involved,' Nathan added.

James turned to Nathan.

'But how involved? They were not merely a side enemy in this war. The Xank were the true decoy. Do you remember that Immortal that I apparently killed in Galis?'

A few of the Troopers nodded.

'It was no Immortal. What I killed in the escape from Galis was none other than an Imperial scout. They were plotting the invasion the entire time.'

Worry seemed to permeate into the crowd.

'Why'd Imperials invade Zona Nox?'

'Because,' James' voice grew in volume, 'Zona Nox wasn't their true target…'

A loud beep echoed throughout the room, drawing James' speech to a close.

At this moment, the crowd of Troopers realised that every hallway was blocked by the yellow Troopers. Murmurs erupted until a regal figure appeared on a platform at the end of the hall.

Dedelux was a tall man sporting a dark grey goatee and sleek, oily hair. His Trooper armour was pitch black and streaked with the ceremonial red of Mars. His cape held a strange yellow emblem, looking somewhat like a crown of nails with a yellow rose in the middle.

The murmurs continued until a woman wearing the yellow armband shouted. 'Silence!'

All murmuring stopped and Dedelux seemed to smirk. He took the microphone away from the woman and spoke in a voice reminiscent of a priest crossed with a drill instructor.

'Troopers of Zona Nox! You have made an exodus from your planet without warning or order from High Command. Your Commanders and Generals have not arrived and I fear that they have been waylaid by Xank. I fear this but do not despair. You have come to safe harbour. This is not a barbaric world like that which you have left. We are civilized and advanced. This is Nova Zarxa, the jewel of Extos III. It is unfortunate that your Planetary General Luci Kareon was unable to be here today, but you will find that I am a passable leader. I am the highest authority here on Nova Zarxa, besides that of our corporate allies in Gragtec. Officers, you will answer to me. Platoons will be reshuffled and one by one, you will be sent back to the homeworld for reassignment.'

There was some coughing in the crowd, but no response. It seemed reasonable enough to Nathan. General Kareon was a somewhat laissez-faire general but Nathan had fought under stricter commanders before. He was used to military orders.

Then Dedelux's tone changed.

'Many civilians have arrived on my planet. Many of them came months before now, fearing Xank occupation but the more recent, those to arrive by corporate ship or by your earlier vessels, claim to be survivors of what they call a 'dead world.' These refugees have been corrected, of course. The planet, Zona Nox, is not dead but merely conquered…'

'Skite-eating rubbish!' a Trooper from across the room shouted.

As many turned to look at him, already two yellow-banded Troopers were restraining him. Murmuring and tensions were growing alongside the swearing of the man.

'Enough!' Dedelux shouted, immediately quelling the crowd with his overly loud voice amplifier.

'Enough,' he repeated, more quietly. 'Let the Trooper speak. We are all brothers here. He deserves a voice.'

The Yellows, as Nathan now referred to them, let go of Lt. Frank McGraff. The Lieutenant straightened himself and then spoke loudly enough so most could hear him. The acoustics in the room were designed to shift according to speaker, so an audio spotlight was now being shone on the irate officer.

'I saw the clouds. You can' tell me otherwise. They was black clouds. No – not clouds. A blanket of darkness covering the sky. General Kareon told us to evacuate and we did. She told us that they were Imperials in Titan. Terra-damn Imperials! You mean to tell me that the sky went black, with Imperials at our gates, and it ain't a dead world?'

Everyone was thinking it, but nobody had the guts to say it. *Thank the Tribal for having guts!* Everyone from Zona Nox was nodding in agreement. The yellows didn't make a move.

Then Dedelux laughed. It sounded good natured but the situation was inappropriate. Its condescension was palpable.

'Imperials? This close to the Outer Reach? I think not. Zona Nox was always a backwater. Don't let the superstition of all-powerful cults rub off on you. The sky didn't go black and the Imperials didn't invade. Our scouting fleets have surveyed the planet and have found that it has been completely taken over by the Xank, but it is still liveable. What we need now is not fear of some empire light-years away, but vigilance against the enemy at our doorstep. I implore you, Troopers of Zona Nox, to remain rational. Only reason and dedication to the Trooper banner will keep Nova Zarxa safe! And obedience! Do not forget obedience. Our might comes from our unity. Do not stray from the Trooper creed. Remain loyal to humanity and obey your superiors.'

Lt. Frank shook his head. 'You expec' me to believe that? I saw it with me own eyes. I don' doubt what I see.'

'Lies permeate the soul and eyes, Trooper. I care not for lies or deception. I also hope that you will not spread this lie to your brothers.'

'I will spread the truth as I want, guvna. Trooper creed and all dat.'

'So can I say that you are disobeying a direct order?'

'You can say what ya want. I saw what I saw.'

Dedelux turned to the yellows flanking the lieutenant.

'Arrest him for suspicion of conspiracy to commit mutiny.'

The yellow lunged for the lieutenant who was too stunned to react.

Outrage erupted throughout the hall and many Troopers made an aggressive move not only towards the yellows but to Dedelux himself.

'Silence!'

The room stopped once again.

'Do not forget, Troopers, that this is not your parish. I am your host and you are my guests. You are here by my charity alone. Lest you forget – I, Triguim Dedelux, am your current master and will be so until you are sent back to the homeworld.

'Dismissed!'

❖

Many a Trooper turned to James as Dedelux spouted lie atop lie. Some of them had pleading eyes. They had expressions which told more than their lips ever could. They were afraid. Afraid of the unknown but, above all, afraid that they were to be relegated the title of liar. Only minutes before, James had claimed that Imperials were the cause and now everything he had claimed was being disputed by a Trooper leader. The Troopers didn't know whom to choose. A decorated commanding officer, or someone who deserved to be decorated?

Many stares almost brought him to speak, but the actions of the accented Trooper made him think better. Dedelux, for all his talk about Trooper creed, was a zot. He preached allowing 'brothers' to speak but at the same time stated his superiority while chastising and arresting said brother. Dedelux was scum, but James knew that some of the biggest scum in the world were also the most powerful. James was not stupid enough to risk his neck. He could not afford interrogation. He had too many secrets to risk revealing.

As the Troopers shuffled out after being dismissed, Nathan sidled up to James and whispered.

'I heard from a boy named Tim that you met Marshal Rekkie.'

'Tim?' James asked, truly astonished. 'Did he make it back?'

'Sure did. I saved him myself in Red Sand. He was with a tank and a Vacaraptor. The Vacaraptor saved my life at Fort Nox. But tell me, how did you meet the Slayer of Ganymede?'

'Accident, really…one of the men with me was shot in the leg by him and he felt apologetic. We did a favour for him and he did some favours for us. He's a very good man.'

'Did he help you off the planet?'

James hesitated. 'That is a story I want to tell you but can't risk being overheard. He did help but I will have to leave it at that.'

Nathan frowned but then smiled. They were in separate lines for registration and they were about to part ways.

'That can be a story for another time then. I'm glad you're okay.'

They were about to part ways completely when James put his hand on Nathan's shoulder.

'I'm glad you're okay too…and…and thanks for saving me in Galis. I will never be able to repay you for that.'

Nathan smiled sadly. 'You won't have to.'

"Our existence has reached a peak where almost all we need to know can be known. As a result, the most terrifying thing in the world is something we don't know." – Henry Urlog, Martian Philosopher

Chapter 7. <u>Knives in the Dark</u>

Danny wasn't scared of the dark. Mob bosses and criminals were not allowed to fear where they belonged. Sure, many gangsters did fear the shadows. The leader of the Purgers, for instance. Danny had reliable intel to suggest that he slept with a night light. That would also account for why the Purgers were seldom allowed out at night.

Even so, many lied about their fears, Danny did not. He feared what any reasonable person did. He feared death, he feared pain and he feared obscurity. Yet, he knew that for one in a career such as his, the first two were inevitable.

Danny did not fear the dark and even the sounds of scuffling in the unseen corners of the room.

He was tied to a chair; that much he knew. He had been knocked out again once the vehicle had stopped. He did not know where he was – if that would help on this planet – or who had taken him. All he knew was that his life was not in his hands anymore. He had his doubts that Aegis would come to save him, but Big Momma had come to surprise him in the past.

Danny's eyes felt as if they had popped as a bright white light shone directly into his face.

Memories of a past interrogation of this nature came back to him. Of course, it had been him giving the interrogation, not taking it. He remembered what he had ordered back then and he couldn't help but shudder now.

The light was too bright for Danny to see. It was for the torturer's benefit, not his own.

'Danny Marzio…crime boss of Galis City. Capital of Red Sands, northern hemisphere of the now dead world…Zona Nox.'

The voice was ominous and possessed the grainy undertones typical of radio intercoms. Its deep tone was obviously the product of a voice modulator. Danny would have no idea who his captors were.

The voice said nothing afterwards until Danny realised that it was in fact a question. He chose not to respond.

Danny heard the zap before he felt it. A zap, a spark and searing vibrating pain shooting through his entire body. He felt as if his bones were seeking to tear out of his skin. He would have screamed if his muscles weren't so tired from the pain.

'You will respond when spoken to…are you Danny Marzio?'

The electricity had stopped and Danny was breathing heavily. With a stutter, he answered. 'Yes.'

'Why are you on Nova Zarxa?'

'I am a refugee…'

Shocks travelled through Danny once again. Like knives piercing his inner flesh, he could only shiver with pain. This time he did let out a scream. It came out as a stammer as his teeth clattered together.

'We do not appreciate lying, Mr Marzio. We can shock you all day without killing you. This torture will only end when you give us the information that we need.'

The electrocution halted and Danny once again fell into frantic panting as his body felt the relief of not having gods know how many volts running through it.

'Let's try another question. Did you attempt to kill Planetary CEO Mark Dresner of the Zerian Corporation?'

This was something that Danny was not afraid to admit.

'Yes.'

'Why?'

'He collaborated with rival gangs to bring down both my gang and the gang of my cousin.'

Danny heard some mumbling over the intercom.

'Another question. Do you know a Gloria Maryan? Codenamed "Big Momma".'

Danny did not respond, at first. He knew what was coming but somehow felt that this was some of the information he needed to keep secret.

Before his interrogators could electrocute him, he replied.

'I have heard the name. She was spoken about at the moot in Titan.'

'Our intelligence suggests that she was at the moot. Are you lying to us, Mr Marzio?'

Skite, they had someone inside the Titan gangs. Danny needed to watch what he said from now on.

'There was a big black lady at the meeting. I was not sure if that was, or was not, the fabled Big Momma.'

That answer seemed to satisfy them.

'Let's go back to an earlier question – seeing as you seem much more willing to answer. What are you doing here on Nova Zarxa?'

'I was given passage by the Titan City Conglomerate as they were escaping the planet.'

'That is a how, not a why.'

'I did not really have a choice in coming here…'

The shocks seemed to echo each other. It was not like being shot or stabbed but rather like one continuous pressure being applied to all his nerves.

'You are in the possession of Aegis bonds as well as seen entering orbit from the Aegis flagship Athena. Are you, Don Marzio, working for the Aegis Corporation?'

Danny did not reply.

His jaw ached. He wanted to scream. He could not.

The shocks continued. Then there was black.

"The use of Warpmancy is both scientific and spiritual. It is based off scientific laws and physics but possesses and requires the will of spirit. While scientists believe they have mastered the theory of the Warp, they have not come close to understanding its use by Warpmancers." - Anonymous

Chapter 8. __Training__

'You need to focus your energy. Exert your will and dominate it in such a way that you can never lose control.'

James did as he was told but this only added to his excruciating headache. It did not come as easily to him as on the Lector ship. In fact, he could hardly lift a mug.

Krag-Zot didn't seem surprised. He said that James' power was because of stored energy. Without the reserves, he had to rely on Warp crystals – which he currently had none.

It had been a day since James had deserted the Zona Nox Troopers. It was not hard to see that the Zonian Troopers were not welcome here. He had utilised the remainder of his Warp reserves to cover his retreat before registration. From there, he had retreated to his Grag-Tec accommodation among the silver-clad towers of this world's corporation. The next morning, Krag-Zot had appeared once again. James did not attempt to argue with the Areq and agreed promptly to begin training.

'How can I use my power if I have none?' James panted, trying to distract Krag-Zot so he could take a break.

'We all have latent power,' Krag-Zot said, as if he had said it a thousand times before (and from what James could tell, he probably had), 'With enough willpower, we can summon up even the smallest reserves into storms.'

This sparked James' interest.

'Besides telekinetic and manipulating gas, what else could I possibly do?'

Krag-Zot thought for a few seconds, creating a mental list.

'Warpmancy is the manipulation of the matter. You can use it to manipulate almost any element if you have some sort of understanding of it. You can also use it as direct power, turning it physical. Imperial energy weapons use the Warp to generate heat. With enough Warp power, you could possibly change the fabric of a world.'

'Terraform it?'

'Yes.'

'Even remove Blight?'

A shadow seemed to rise over Krag-Zot.

'No…well…technically yes. But the cost is too great. Much too great.'

James was curious but didn't press. This was an issue they both were victims of but Krag-Zot had lived untold years feeling bitter about.

'Now, Boymancer,' Krag-Zot announced, yet again back in the role as mentor, 'let's create a spark.'

James focused his mind and held his Conduit glove in front of him. He sensed the energy all around him. Warp was everywhere. In the air, in the furniture, walls and even in him. It was everywhere, like moisture in humid air. It was not enough to start a flood, but James would have to try. He had never had to rely on such a miniscule amount of energy at his disposal.

He let out his will, seeking to dominate the energy around him – just to have it slip out of his fingers.

'Don't just grasp at it without purpose. You're not some barbarian fisherman in a stream. Figure out your goal. Order the powers of the Warp. Give it purpose!'

James stopped grasping. Purpose? How do you give objects a purpose? Then something clicked.

With a mental shout, James commanded the energy around him. 'Ignite!'

A spark bellowed into a ball of fire right in front of him. Defying all laws of logic, it stayed motionless in the shape of a sphere, exactly at the point where he had ordered it to.

James felt a sense of identity emanate from it. A sense of value and a connection to him – its creator and shaper.

'Well done. You are not just some army trained telekineticist. You have the promise to be a true Warpmancer, like that of my people.'

'What's the difference,' James asked, cupping the fire in his hand. He felt its warmth and knew that if it was any other type of fire. He could be burnt – but it was his fire.

'The Imperials train Warpmancers en masse, but they have lost the spiritual importance of true Warpmancy. They are like children flinging mud. You – you have the capacity to be a god.'

There it was again. Krag-Zot was calling him a god. *How can I be a god if I don't even believe in one?*

'They call you an Immortal,' James asked, changing the topic, 'do you truly live forever?'

'Nothing lasts forever – but for my purpose, I do.'

'How did you become this way?'

Krag-Zot didn't reply immediately. A crease seemed to cross his brow and his underbite rose slightly.

'Warpmancy. I gave everything to the Warp and it gave me eternity.'

James stared at the Areq, giving him a look from head to toe. He hadn't noticed it before, but the only exposed flesh on Krag-Zot was his head. The rest was cybernetic.

'You're part android?'

'It becomes easier to control the Warp when you can use your entire body as a conduit. I gave up my worldly flesh lifetimes ago.'

'Does the machinery prevent your body from aging?'

'Yes, but that is not what makes me Immortal. Even if I lived in a body of flesh – it would still decay. My spirit is what is Immortal.'

'What happens when your body dies?'

'Before that happens, I utilise the Warp to transfer my consciousness to a new body. That typically requires a full body Conduit, however, which would make a flesh body unable to undertake the task.'

'So you can pretty much live forever?'

'Yes – yes, I could.'

Krag-Zot's mood seemed to sink. He looked away from James into a mirror on the apartment wall.

'You sacrifice much more than limbs to become what I am. You sacrifice your own life. You can never die peacefully, no matter how much you may wish it. I am a warrior at heart, but sometimes I wish for a quiet end. Sometimes, I just wish it all to end.'

'Why don't you end it all yourself?'

There was a pause, then Krag-Zot looked into James' eyes. 'Because I am afraid.'

The revelation didn't shock James but it seemed to send shockwaves through what had previously seemed a figure of stoicism.

'I've lived for so long,' Krag-Zot continued, 'while so many else have died. Do I deserve this? Doesn't matter.

What does matter – is that I'm afraid of what will happen when I finally die.'

'Everyone is afraid of death…'

'Not Immortals – we're supposed to have overcome that fear. We are endless.'

'Then why become Immortals?'

That seemed to catch Krag-Zot's interest.

'Why become immortal if you don't fear death? I would think that the only reason. Even if you live forever – the fact that you chose to become that way means you fear dying.'

They both remained quiet for a while after until James broke the silence.

'What's the next lesson?'

'No more Warpmancy today. I can see your head is getting sore. Instead, I want to accustom you to a strong possibility. Sit…'

James did as instructed. Krag-Zot did the same.

'I respect you, Boymancer. I may be your mentor but I can see a spark in you which is something I'd willingly follow. Many others would do the same. You need to come to terms with that. Many will want to follow you and many will want to die for you. Are you comfortable with that?'

Am I? James had thought about it before but it was still something he struggled to grasp. Smith and Marshal had mentioned an Aura of Authority caused by his Warpmancy – but that was gone now. He had run out of his Warp reserves. Yet people still looked to him. The Troopers in the hall, his comrades from Zona Nox and even this Areq – a being who had tried to kill him.

'Do people follow me because of my skill? Why? What do people see in me?'

'You are a boy of many talents and respectable prowess – but many an elite soldier is. You are a good warrior, but not the best. No. People follow you because you keep on going. When lesser men would curl up and give up, you persevere. You are not a leader because you are powerful – you are a leader because you do not allow people to give up. Remember that.'

James nodded. He would.

'What do I do? People follow me but I don't know what I'm supposed to be doing myself. Smith says I need to avenge my people. I want that vengeance – I really do…but how? I don't know where to start.'

'This isn't only your fight. Your homeworld and the birthplace of your species were all human worlds. They were lost to the same enemy – all humans have the right to fight that enemy.'

'They don't know about it…'

'And that is what you will change.'

Krag-Zot walked towards the apartment window and gazed out the one-way glass. He watched as the city-life of Nova Zarxa began as flying cars darted between towers. Below, a cold glow rose from the crystal mining below.

'You will be that change,' he continued. 'I call you a potential god and I really mean it. Every people needs a messiah. Your Terra is an archaic ideology clinging to old hope and ill-suited solutions. Your people need a new symbol. You have been wronged. I have been wronged. The Empire of Xank was founded to avenge the destruction of our world Resh – but we became as bad as the Imperials. This new crusade must not be a hollow desire for revenge and blood.

'No, Boymancer – you will be a symbol of hope, justice and progress. You will be the messiah that my people lacked. You will lead your people against their own oppressors. Dedelux will fall by the people. Zerian. The Gangs. Even the Troopers. All will mean nothing. You will re-shape the galaxy – until finally, you free your worlds.'

James was terrified as Krag-Zot spoke.

'What if I don't want to be their messiah? Why can't they find their own way? They have a right to run their own lives.'

'Do they do that now?'

That gave James pause.

'They wake up, work, breed and die. This is the way it has always been. They live in tedium with drugs – chemical and otherwise – giving them the occasional meaning. Would you withhold from them something more? Your people deserve more. Under the Xank, I helped enslave billions. We created slaves out of species, but what I realised the most was how willing they were to become one. They fought, they lost and they accepted their loss. Under us, they were given purpose. They were slaves – but better than any servant. They were involved in a crusade.'

'But people have a right to be free.'

'Freedom can only be given. It cannot be attained by oneself – no slave can unfasten their own chains. Your people – the people on this blighted rock, once my home – are slaves. You will free them. One is only free with purpose. You will give them purpose.'

Krag-Zot turned to James, who was now sitting back in his chair, unable to speak.

'You will be a symbol - a god – and they will call you Defiant!'

"Liberty is dangerous. Prisons have safety. Dictators are stagnant and known. Liberty is chaos. Liberty is the unknown. Liberty is what every society deserves – a bright and vibrant future of uncertainty and wonder." – Jeffan Grouger, Ganymede Activist

Chapter 9. <u>Freedom</u>

Defiance is what the people of Zeruit needed. It was what Leri required of them. The Zangorian thought this as he stood on the precipice of a hill overlooking Bexong.

The settlement was but a hamlet compared to what Leri had encountered in his career as a Word Lectorate soldier – but was apparently the home of the rebels Leri needed to start his revolution.

Leri was not afraid of being seen standing on the hilltop. He wore his red cape – the very same taken from the battlefield at Fort Nox. He stood with his flesh arm by his side, his new arm clutching a Kuru, a traditional Zangorian spear. He stood on the edge of the grassy knoll, watching the Zangorian workers below. Each one carried a pipe linked up to a barrel on their backs.

They trudged down the long lines of upturned soil, poking the tip of their pipes into the soil to suction out the juicy worms below. This was the main form of agriculture that the Zangorian war-machine relied upon. Patrolling the fields and further on were groups of hovering drones. Each drone possessed a single cyclops eye and a single arm. When a worker slacked off or misbehaved, the drone would deliver a shock to them. The shock could be adjusted to different severities. Many of the workers simply jolted but Leri watched as a few were flung back, twitching.

According to Peron, the villagers seemed to believe that the drones were the ultimate authority – and in many ways, they may have been. Many of these Zangorians had been born into this community and had known nothing else. The drones were their overseers – unspeaking overseers. They undertook their job and loaded the tramways because of habit and fear, nothing more.

Leri leapt off his perch and began surfing down the hill. Some workers must have heard him as they lifted their beaks.

Multiple clicks and squawks followed.

'Who is it?'

'Outsider?'

'Don't look, the overseers will hurt you.'

Leri continued his advance, unperturbed. He landed upon solid ground with a jolt. He used his Kuru to steady his landing and then propel him forward towards the closest drone. Before the robot could react, the point of the spear had impaled it and then left. Leri turned and spun, smacking a drone behind him with full force, denting its side and destroying its vitals.

No worker continued harvesting the worms. Their eyes were all fixed on this stranger destroying their oppressors.

All the drones, detecting the danger, charged towards him. They spoke in robotic emotionless voices.

'Stranger, you are in an unauthorised area – identify yours…'

Just to be smashed or stabbed or kicked or punched. Even when the drone AI realised he was a foe, their attempts at electrocuting him were to no avail.

Wires shot out at him were easily dodged and every bot that came past the range of his spear met his steel-clad talon. The dirt surrounding him was becoming a heap of beeping, smoking, charred metal – yet more drones kept coming. They were weak and Leri could dispatch each one easily – but there were so many.

He was tiring. A drone shot a wire at him and just as he dodged, he felt a sharp stab as he was shocked by a drone to his rear. The pain was excruciating. He tried to steady himself, but he could not help but shake.

The drones were surrounding him. Then he heard a shout. A battle cry.

'Rii!' a myriad of voices shouted in unison – as drones began to fall.

Orange feathered arms tore at metallic limbs. Beaks hit steel and zaps contrasted with squawks and squeals. The drones turned to ignore Leri.

'Get back to your work…' a drone said, just before being torn apart by two young Zangorians, as if the drone was a rope in tug-of-war.

Eventually, there was only silence.

Every drone was disabled, left smoking in heaps. Leri remained crouched as countless beady eyes stared at him with awe.

'Make way!' a creaky voice sounded above the quiet.

The voice belonged to a grey Zangorian possessing many ruffled feathers, including a wisp of them below his beak – like what humans called beards.

'I am the Elder of Bexong, stranger. My name is Gura-Teng. What can I call our liberator?'

Leri looked up at him and remembered what the people had shouted. 'Rii' – Freedom. It was apt a name as any.

'My name is Rii and I have come to free my people.'

❖

The hall was filled with a joy that Leri knew they had never experienced before. The sights, sounds and taste of the air itself was that of elation and hope. One would normally feel quite silly to think of happiness and joy having a taste and smell but Leri experienced all of it here in Bexong.

Men (for there were only men in Bexong) and male children sang and danced. They shared beverages and stories of their short but successful revolution.

Gura-Teng was speaking to Leri, or Rii. He liked the name. His real name was a symbol of his past life, meaning 'waiting to be free' while his new name was a sign of his willingness to fight for a new world. A world of freedom,

'We got by in Bexong,' Gura-Teng was saying, 'but it was never a life. The metal-lords ruled us and hurt us. They never killed us but they didn't have to. Sometimes we killed ourselves. They never took our lives but they had already eliminated our ability to live. Thank you, once again, for freeing us…Rii.'

Leri did not reply for a while. He continued to watch. The joyful faces of the children were what caught his eyes. His only memory of children was from his past lives. He remembered joy there but not in his own existence. There was a big difference between remembering and seeing. To Leri, the expressions on these youths' faces were liberating.

'Do not thank me till you are truly free,' Leri replied. For there was still much to do. 'Your people are not the only slaves. Your metal-overlords were but pawns. What do you know of your oppression?'

Gura-Teng looked slightly taken aback, the tufts of greying feathers underneath his beak swayed as he took in a deep breath.

'I have lived for a long time, much longer than my kin usually survive. In that time, I have learnt one thing above all – how little I actually know.

'From what I do know – the metal-lords, as you said, were just pawns. We have had the dark walkers investigate our homes before. They are the ones who take us in the night and then return us to our homes the next day. It has happened to all of us, but we do not remember what they did to us. There was seldom violence – we never put up a fight.'

Unfortunately, Leri did know what the 'dark walkers' did to the men of this village. They milked them for their seed so to breed more Zangorian soldiers and labourers. This was the life of a serf – they lived for labour and their seed.

'There is much more to life than this, you know.'

'We heard rumours from the occasional supply caravan – when we still got caravans. Now everything is sped in by those metal tracks. Last stranger here came when I was a child.'

Leri was once again reminded of the total insular nature of these villages. The people of Zeruit, his people, were treated like machines. They had a function and no permission to stray from that mission. It was…disgusting.

Leri knocked over his stool as he stood up. The thud of wood on stone somehow managed to silence the music and attract everyone else's attention.

As everyone stared, Leri spoke.

'Zangorians – my kindred, my brothers – I am Rii. In your tongue, this is called Freedom – Liberator. As my name commands, I am here to free you…all of you…'

A few Zangorian men whooped in excitement but the majority remained quiet.

'I cannot claim credit for throwing down your metal-overlords. That was you. You chose to pick up stick, shovel and rock and use them to undo centuries of dictatorship. I may have kicked the rock but all of you are responsible for causing the landslide. For this, I cannot claim responsibility for freeing you.

'I have come to this planet – our home – to retract a great wrong. I have come to FREE our people!'

This time, a much larger group gave out cheers. Leri let them cheer before he silenced them with a wave of his mechanical arm.

'There are thousands, if not hundreds of thousands, of villages just like Bexong on this planet. Each and every one, ruled by our oppressors. Dark walkers, metal-overlords and much more stand in our way…'

This silenced the group. It seemed many hadn't thought of this before.

'They will stand in our way,' Leri repeated, 'they will try to stop the tides of freedom. They will try to enslave us or slaughter us. They have weapons capable of wiping out peoples thousands greater than us.'

Fear now gripped the group. Even Gura-Teng was leaning back in his chair, gripping the armrests until his talons made scratches.

'They will stand in our way – I say, let 'em! Our people have lived far too long in servitude. I say it's time to fight. Not to keel over and beg. Not to apathetically let them deny us our futures and families. They will stand in our way. We will push them right over!'

Everyone stood. Trills and cheers and whoops and shouts of agreement drowned out all other sounds. Men turned to each other, hyping each other up. Children, unable to understand most of what Leri said, picked up on the excitement and were cheering too.

Gura-Teng was the only one not smiling.

'You have sent my people to their death.'

Leri spoke to him without looking.

'Better to die free than live another moment a slave.'

Gura-Teng nodded but didn't smile. The old Zangorian knew of necessity, he just didn't like it. Bexong would fight for freedom. Bexong would fight and Leri would lead them.

"We persevere." – Red Sand rancher, North of Galis Lake.

Chapter 10. <u>New Struggles</u>

Extos III rose across the horizon, bathing the silver towers of Nexus in a warm glow. The night was over. Day-ports began to open their metal shutters, blue energy shields activating to keep out the toxins of the cold outside. Their night-port cousins remained open, while some closed for the day. Different buildings needed to take turns to conserve energy. This was the way of Nexus. Without the understated blue shields, the populace would choke on Warp poison. Without the oxygen filtration systems, they would suffocate. Without generators and a strict energy regimen, all of this would fail. Nexus was a shining, seeming utopia, stifled by a poisoned atmosphere.

Zonians arriving on this harsh world of glitz and prosperity found none. They were a people of grit. Their struggles were under an open sky – not the geradite ceilings of Nexus City. Even the occupants of Titan City found themselves ill at ease. The skyscrapers were like home, but were somehow wrong. They were not places of ambition.

The corporate survivors felt stifled. The corporate and security monopoly prevented entrepreneurship. Only those used to humble lives didn't feel the repression, until they started looking for work.

No Zonian waited to look for work. They knew their lot and the fact that their currency was worthless in this neighbour planet. Grag-Tec recruited some Zonians, but there was simply not enough work under the corporation. Other Zonians looked for odd jobs. They were by no means unskilled. A life in the barrens of Red Sand or the streets of Galis did not train a soft people. They filled peasants with grit, and trained a warrior society.

When the Zonians arrived, they did not understand the noisy nightclubs of Nexus. They did not understand the sense dulling drugs. Drugs were meant to enhance performance, not dull it. They didn't understand when people told them that they were filthy parasites. They had never heard the term. They didn't understand why they were rejected from every place of business, even though each possessed a help wanted sign. They were a doing people, being disallowed from activity. When you take away a man's right to work, you force him to become a criminal.

When the people of Zona Nox were not allowed the ability to earn their keep, they resorted to what the Galisians knew best. They stole. They hid in the shadows, mugging those who had spat on them. They looted stores and storerooms for food and gas. No place would sell them accommodation, so they lived as nomads, camping in the hallways of the city, dodging patrols.

Zonians never felt united on their homeworld, but now they fought as a common people. Zenite watched Marzio backs. Titan-dwellers gave food to Red Sanders. Dead Stoners helped the children of Tribals. The diverse people of Zona Nox were no longer that. They were Zonians, united by pain. They lived together, fought together and disappeared one by one. Those Zonians cunning enough to hide their identities watched on, impotently, as their countrymen disappeared off the shining hallways of Nexus, no longer marring the perfect façade of Extos III's greatest city.

❖

James did not have to avoid any Yellow Trooper patrols on his walk from his apartment to the Grag-Tec office. The newly married Exanoid couple next door had gone off-world for a honeymoon on Eran. The lack of music gave

James a blissful morning. He now knew it to be morning, as he had asked a Zarxian Gray to set a notification system for him on his watch. It still told Zona Nox time, but was set to vibrate at certain times, to indicate the correct time of day in Nexus. Krag-Zot had warned him the day before that this would be a free day for him. He wished James to find his bearing in this new place.

'A prince must learn of his domain,' Krag-Zot had recited, quoting something. James didn't ask.

The Grag-Tec headquarters was only one of many Grag-Tec facilities on the planet, but the only one which didn't receive any patrols from Yellows. Instead, the Grag-Tec HQ was patrolled by Merka, Gray and Trooper-mercenary guards. James felt safe around them, as he had already become acquainted with many.

James greeted a Merka named Maka'ru before entering the administration offices of Grag-Tec. He had an appointment with a friend and was allowed in immediately.

Ryan beamed as he looked up from his paperwork.

'James! Didn't think I'd see you so soon.'

James accepted the now standing Ryan's handshake, grasping one another's wrists. Ryan indicated for him to sit.

'So, they got you working already? It's only been two days!'

Ryan blushed. 'Well, it seems I already got the basics. I wrote an exam. Mathematics, accountancy…all that. Aced it.'

'Congrats! Not like one of us Galisians to pass an exam. You doing us all proud.'

Ryan waved away the compliment.

'Seems ranchers need all the skills an Overseer does. My bookkeeping for pa sure helped.'

'You never did tell me all about your past…never mind. Not my business.'

'No, no. I owe you that much, Captain. I was born on a ranch by Galis Lake, the green side. My family owned a ranch. We raised Mozar and Peckers…was a good life. My pa trained me to be a rancher. Not just some dumb farmhand, but with numbers. I'd fill in the registry – oversee trades. It was fun. The greatest feeling was when my pa would nod approvingly at my spreadsheets. He'd smile and say, "That's my boy."'

'What happened? How you become a gangster?'

'First time I killed was as a rancher,' Ryan continued. 'A Red City bandit was rustling our biggest bull. My dad was in Galis. I was the only one who could save Big Harry. I took my dad's rifle from the shed and shot the bandit in the head. I vomited after that. My dad was angry when he got home. He wasn't angry at me. Just angry. He didn't want me shooting things. Said he wanted more for me. A year after that, Dead Stone fell. Refugees flooded into Galis. It went from a spaceport to a sprawling city. But the refugees brought chaos. The local Trooper garrison had to send reinforcements to the city. They weren't able to save my ranch when we were hit by aliens.'

'Xank?'

Ryan shook his head. 'Squogg. They had never been to Zona Nox before. Mercenaries later said it was deserters from the Black Fleet. The fat grakos burnt my ranch to the ground. They killed my sis, my ma and my pa. I was the only one left. I was told to run. I didn't look back. I returned with a posse from the other ranches. It was too late.'

There was a pause. James broke it. 'I'm sorry.'

'Don't be,' Ryan smiled sadly. 'It's good to get it off my chest. You don't have the full story yet, though.

'Ranches were falling all around Galis Lake. Troopers couldn't handle the Xank attacks. They started helping ranchers move into Galis and set up urban farming programmes. I followed one of the convoys. I was angry though. I hated the people who had done this to my family and me. When I got to Galis, I didn't join a farm. Farmers didn't change the world, I thought. They didn't get revenge. Farming didn't save my dad or the ranch. Only time we were ever saved was when I put a bullet in that grako bandit's head. Lead and steel changed things. So, I started fighting. I joined a fight ring. Killed some more people. Didn't vomit anymore. Eventually, Don Marzio noticed me and gave me a little more meaning. You generally know the rest.

'But that's all changed now. I'm sick of the shooting and the breaking. I want to farm again. Not literally. But I want to grow something. After I raise funds with Grag-Tec, I want to start a company. It's time that I do some good.'

'I am sure you will, and that company is going to be a force to be reckoned with.'

'I don't care about the power. I just want to it sustain itself – to employ some people. If I can prevent some more farmhands becoming like I did, then I will be happy.'

James nodded. 'You're a good man, Ines Ryan Rebeck.'

Ryan smiled. 'You too, Captain.'

❖

'Zonians are disappearing, James,' Quok announced, pouring a glass of spirits.

'I heard,' James' voice didn't betray any worry.

'I want to prevent any harm coming to you. I owe you that much.'

'Any help would be appreciated.'

Quok nodded and passed James the glass of vodka. He then turned to stare out the window.

'It is so odd…' he took a tip… 'to be back in such a place. The grit, the bloody sand and dirt of Zona Nox was discomforting, but it was honest. Here, we hide our emotions with mind numbing excuses for entertainment. We use metal so that the blood from squatters can be cleaned easily. Yet, it is not even metal. It is a chemical substitute. Nothing in Nexus is what it seems. We are a shining city. We have the most money. We don't starve. Well, that might change with the Xank blockades. But, there's no plagues like on Grengen. There are no bloody memories of genocides like on Glotos III. We aren't a crime ridden cesspool. Yet, why does this all unease me? Perhaps, it is because of the deceit. Zarxians lie to themselves. They deafen themselves on bad alien music. They take drugs that make them pass out. They hate their lives so much that they don't even want to be conscious. Yet, they claim to be superior. Jewel of Extos III my rump.'

Quok turned to James, slightly wobbly from the booze. 'The only happy Zarxian is a rebel, James. You can't be happy in a place like this. These shining walls clamp down on us. They press in, harsher and harsher. Tighter and tighter. The repression is palpable. How can I rule over a place like this? How can I tell my employees that they have to leave the only homes they've ever known? I promised them safety. I promised them an honest living. Dedelux has made me a liar. An Exanoid is as good as his word… I am nothing.'

James winced as Quok, who was now just in front of him, permeated the air with the smell of strong spirits. Evidently, the Exanoid had been drinking long before James had arrived.

'Grag-Tec rules over Nova Zarxa by name alone. Dedelux, by force of arms, reigns as prince,' Quok slurred.

'Yet, I owe my people. Grag-Tec is a family, and we don't abandon our own.'

'Neither do Zonians,' James interrupted. 'I have hidden in the shadows as my people have been wasting away. I fear, however, that I need to hide for a bit longer. I need help. Give me a job at Grag-Tec. I will repay the favour. I will help you keep your word.

Quok nodded and then waved James off.

James stood up and left, the final scene of the room being Quok pouring yet another cup of vodka, muttering to himself.

'I hate this planet.'

"Freedom isn't about restraints. It's about will. You aren't free for lack of shackles, but because you refuse to be a slave." – Gert the Agitator

Chapter 11. <u>Anticipation</u>

There was one thing Nathan hated more than a contact. That was waiting for it. Waiting for an ambush, for a Trooper, epitomised the whole human condition. In minutes, an hour or even days, a Trooper examined their whole life, all while waiting for death. An ambush, even if you survived, was death. You lost friends. You lost associates. You lost your innocence. Waiting for a contact was waiting to die.

The mood in the mess hall these past days was that of awaiting death. Food was eaten, games were played and people chatted, but a dark cloud hovered over all of them.

Lt Frank McGraff didn't return to his squad. Nobody dared ask for an explanation. No trial had taken place. Frank, the blustering officer, was now merely a whisper.

Every entrance of the mess hall was flanked by armed Zarxian military police. No one left without permission. Like children or prisoners, they were not allowed out of the military district.

Every afternoon, another platoon was shipped off – sent back to Mars for re-assignment. No one could question this. Of course, this didn't stop the whispers.

'Why send us away?'

'Xank at our doorstep.'

'No, Imperials at our doorstep. Zarxa will be defenceless.'

'Dedelux is moronic.'

'Is he? I think this is what he wants.'

'For Zarxa to fall…'

Every so often, one of these whisperers disappeared. As such, Nathan chose not to speak unnecessarily. He ate, he occasionally played poker and he drank. Many a familiar face was now disappearing but the face most absent was one that didn't appear in the mess hall or barracks at all.

James.

Nathan had searched for him all over. No Trooper who knew him had seen him. He simply did not appear. There was no record of him on any directory viewable by Nathan. It was as if he wasn't even a Trooper.

This ghostly nature of James, coupled with the complete mystery of the outside world terrified Nathan. The Zona Nox troopers were blind to all around them. Despite their tenacity and professionalism, this lack of intel visibly shook them.

Frustration had reached breaking point many times over the past week and fights had become common. Cabin fever and fear was the order of the day.

Nathan looked out over the crowd of red and black. Faces wore expressions of bleak greyness.

'Oh, James – wherever you are, at least it's not here.'

❖

James had never thought that he'd be getting a pay check for handling paperwork. He wasn't going to lie, he'd rather be storming an enemy position, or flinging furniture around than his current job but as he settled in, it became quite therapeutic.

Quok had been more than willing to forge the proper data entry for James. It wasn't precisely lying. According to Quok, James was pretty much an honouree member of Grag-Tec already.

James' new title gave him a unique authority in Nexus. He was still a Trooper but was not bound by the Dedelux administration but rather the rule of Grag-Tec.

The Troopers, for the most part, were a charity organisation devoted to protecting humans around the galaxy. To fund their endeavours and campaigns, they often sold mercenary contracts to many corporations. James had been assigned as one such mercenary to Grag-Tec. He now wore a black urban law enforcement uniform with green stripes on the shoulders and a Grag-Tec logo on the chest. He carried a Grag-Tec stun gun and an automatic pistol. Compared to his usual kit, he felt drastically under dressed. Little could be done about that though. He was technically still a Trooper and thus a soldier but Nexus was not like Galis. It was a civilised place. Unlike Galis, there was a government here, and from what James had seen of said government, he was unimpressed.

Propaganda and tasteless effigies declaring the virtue of the governor were everywhere. His personal Trooper army patrolled the streets merely to punish detractors. The atmosphere of trade and prosperity was an illusion for far-reaching oppression. James was not going to be caught dead unable to do anything about it. Despite this not being his town or even his planet, this was now James' home. He felt for its people, but more so for his own.

The refugees of Zona Nox still flooded into Nexus and the bordering mining outposts. Even the prohibition against refugees had not stemmed the tide. The first wave was only that from Fort Nox – more and more arrived by the day in slower vessels. All came bearing the same news: black clouds of death, no air, corruption, and no life – Blight.

Dedelux's personal body-baggers made sure that those with the biggest mouths kept quiet as soon as they got off the ship – by any means necessary. As a result, the people of James' world kept silent. They couldn't come to terms with what had happened to them. They were lost and destitute. Now the refugees of Zona Nox lay huddled in the warehouses of dead companies, keeping warm by trash fires or dying on cold metal. Many turned to crime but Nexus wasn't like Galis. It was hard escaping down one long hallway.

Grag-Tec was helping keep James' people alive through food parcels and fuel, but it simply wasn't enough. The refugees needed real homes. They needed their planet back.

'Oh, how we have fallen,' a voice came from beside him.

'Without a home, our people are just beggars. Worse off than any homeless junkie back in Galis,' James agreed, nodding to greet Marshal beside him.

'Zona Nox was no paradise but it was our planet. It was a symbol of freedom. Reason I moved back. Zonians are not weak people. We're strong. Our civilisation was built around a mountain range called the Teeth of Storms, for Terra sake. We persevered through the hard times. All of us – the Tribals in the cold and the gunslingers in the desert. We could handle anything. But this…they've clipped our wings.'

That was it really. It wasn't the food running out or the cold during the day and night. It wasn't even the confined living spaces. The refugees had lost their reason for being. They had lost their freedom. No amount of security or health or credits could replace that.

The people of Zona Nox needed their freedom back. They needed someone to give it to them – no, to lead them to it.

'Our people need a leader, Marshal. We never had many in Galis but that doesn't mean we don't need one now. They need a symbol or someone to remind them that they're still alive.'

'Exactly, and you're going to be that leader.'

James snorted until he realised that Marshal was serious.

'I was thinking…you know…more that you should be the leader. You're a damn legend! After all, you're the Red Sand Ranger – the pinnacle of soldiering on the frontier. Why me when they could have you?'

Marshal sighed. 'You overestimate me, my boy. I was a soldier, not a leader. All those missions I was on – just a soldier. I was either alone or taking the orders. I was a good soldier but a good gunman does not a good leader make. Now you, you are someone that I'd follow.'

James was not convinced. Marshal pressed on. Both ignored James' duty of checking cargo for contraband.

'Think about it - all those people who followed you. They were a cross section of Galis. Gangsters, thugs, mechanics, tradesmen, ranchers – if you could lead all those people…together, what makes leading these people any different?'

'There's Terra-knows how many Zonians on this damn frozen rock, Marshal. I'm still a damn teenager. I've led a squad of fighters – not an entire planet.'

'All you need to do is give them hope,' Marshal was whispering now. 'Someone needs to remind them that life is worth living.'

'Why don't you do it?'

'I'm old, worn out. I have a wife and kid now. I'm tired of this skite. It's time for the next generation to take over the fight. I'll see you around sometime. Think on what I said.'

Marshal walked off with no more to say. James did think on it; long and hard.

❖

Aven Smith was sipping his tea when the yellow light on his dashboard started blinking. The light was a signal that someone had landed in the docking bay. Normally this would be no surprise, as Krag-Zot the Immortal would often fly in and out of the Word Lectorate ship with his personal fighter. Krag-Zot, however, was out of the system searching for new agents.

Speaking over the intercom, Aven spoke in flawless Krugari. 'What is going on in the hangar? Is Krag-Zot back?'

'No, Lector. It's…it's an Edal.'

Aven leapt to his feet. *An Edal, here?*

'How did he get in?'

'He had the pass codes. What should we do?'

'Battle stations!'

With that, sirens erupted across the vessel. Aven hastily unlocked his gun cabinet, hands shaking. He pulled out a submachine gun and then ran into the hallway. Many of his Krugar were already in position, hanging from bars on the roof with two of their hands while using the others to hold pulse blasters.

Ahead of them was the door to the main hall. It was locked now, but if the Edal could have gotten into the hangar, he could get through this.

'Everybody hold position. Only fire on my command.'

He didn't need to remind them of protocol – they were better at that than he was. He said it more to comfort himself.

After the final rustling stopped, all was quiet. Quiet enough to hear the footfalls on metal as a figure approached the door. With a few beeps and a click, the door opened.

The Edal stood stunned as he stared at the forces arranged against him. But Aven didn't give the order to fire. Instead, he stood up calmly and lowered his hand.

'Stand down. He's one of us.'

The Edal looked visibly relieved and approached Aven.

'Lector, I am here to give a report.'

'Better be good, Huin. You won't be able to go back after this.'

'It's not good, sir, and that's why I'm here. The Imperials are mustering a huge invasion force.'

'When are they never?'

'I don't think you understand, Lector. They are preparing to invade Nova Zarxa.'

Huin was right. That wasn't good.

❖

James had just entered his apartment back in the Grag-Tec residences when he spotted Aven Smith standing in his room. He was shaking uncontrollably – his already pale skin reduced to that of a paper sheet.

'Lector, didn't expect to see you planet-side,' James stated, dropping his guard-issue weapons onto the coffee table. He had come to expect this sort of thing from the Word Lectorate. Locked doors meant very little to them.

'There's been…a change of plans. We can't wait any longer. We must make our move. Now!'

'What is it? Speak up.'

Aven looked like he was going to be sick. 'One of my spies has come back from Imperial Space. He was only meant to leave under the direst circumstances. And trust me – this is dire. A Martyr-led fleet is converging on Nova Zarxa. He gives us around one to two Zarxian months. Around seventy days, maybe less.'

James had to sit down at this revelation. He knew it was coming, but not this quickly. This changed everything.

'What would you advise we do, Lector?' James finally asked. Aven was also sitting now.

'You will have to warn the planetary governor. I've heard of his corruption but even he should be able to see this threat. I have adjusted evidence here. It is the report my spy gave me, but adjusted to remove mention of the Word Lectorate.'

'What should I say if they ask how I got this?'

'Use your Grag-Tec connections. Ask your friends if you can claim it is from a scouting vessel. That's believable enough…'

The door opened at that moment to reveal Marshal. He was surprised for a moment but then quickly realised the situation – or guessed it.

'The Imperials are closing in?' he asked, stone-faced.

James nodded.

Marshal sighed. 'I knew this was coming. Aven, I trust you have given us sufficient evidence to show the Governor?'

'If he doesn't believe that, he's an Imperial agent,' Aven tried to smile but failed.

'Then let's not waste any more time,' James stood up. 'Marshal, come with me. We need to make an appointment with Dedelux.'

"The basis of all Trooper power is that of security. The Troopers are not builders. They are not bureaucrats. They are soldiers. And like any enlightened military – they know better than intervening in the affairs of peace." – High Protector Winston at the trial of multiple corrupt Trooper commanders

Chapter 12. Hated

Darren did not hesitate to give away his last tank of valathene. He had invested in the tanks with his Titan bonds after his Junker had finally landed in Nexus. The fuel was a common, but necessary, commodity on such a cold planet. He hadn't managed to sell a single tank, but not for lack of trying. Every time he tried to sell the gas to those who could afford it, he was either ignored or chased away by Yellow Troopers. That left his only customer base being his fellow Zonians – who had no money.

In the beginning, the Zonians rented accommodation around the planet and looked for work to subsidise their survival, but that all changed once Dedelux ordered all Zonians into the lower hangars. Soon enough, all Zonians were confined to ghettos. Penniless and without any means of working for credits, the Zonians began to freeze. Darren gave up on offloading the gas for a profit and began handing it to those who needed it. It wasn't like he was going to find a buyer when he wasn't even allowed to go to the market.

'You are a treasure, Mr Peterson,' a middle-aged woman told him, accepting the small tank and handing it to her larger son.

'I do what I must. We all do.'

The woman nodded, forlornly.

'Who could think such a shining city would be so cruel?' she added.

'Titan shone.'

'But the Underbelly was black. It was honest. We didn't have much, but at least we had a reason. If we wanted something, we would get it. We didn't have scumbags holding a gun at us whenever we tried to go to the bathroom. We were free.'

That was it, really. The poverty on Zona Nox was not unlike this, but it wasn't oppressive. People bled, but they were free. They needed freedom to seek the opportunity to survive. On Nexus, they were forbidden the simplest of necessities. Not because they did not work. Not because they were lazy, or enemies. They were denied the very means to their survival because of what they were. Nothing else. But through this alienation, they had started to find comradery among old enemies. They were no longer Galisians, Red Sanders, Titans…they were Zonians.

'Yellows!'

The shouts echoed across the camp. The guards came every once in a while, to make sure Zonians weren't breaking down the walls of the hangar to steal electricity.

Darren nodded goodbye to the nameless mother and son. He didn't fear that his lack of gas would result in starvation or frostbite on his part. You give to your community and they give to you. Credits or not, the Zonians would look out for one another. Even if they had never done so back on their homeworld. Struggle united. He packed his few belongings and sped off around the corner, attempting to stow away in a dark corner to avoid any confrontation.

As he retreated, he heard shouts. The shouts were incomprehensible, but angry. Darren heard crunching and crying. He stopped and started back, almost mindlessly.

'You can't do this! All I own is in there,' the mother from before sobbed.

Yellows were tearing down her shack, not paying any mind to her possessions. Two Zonians held her back, shame in their eyes. Her son, around thirteen, had a feral look about him as he stood to the side.

There were three Yellows. One officer and two new recruits. The officer oversaw the destruction of the plastic hovel, his mask not betraying his sentiments.

As the shack was torn apart, a small picture frame dropped onto the floor. The son pounced to retrieve it, just to be hit back by the officer with a baton.

'Stay where you are, scum,' the officer spat. 'We are evicting all you disease ridden rodents. Zots, all of you. Dedelux has been more than generous. Stay out of our way!'

Zonians jumped at the strike, but didn't advance. Darren watched, his expression unchanging. The son's expression didn't change. He looked mad. His mouth sounded silently, 'Dad.'

Darren didn't say anything when the boy pulled a switchblade from his sleeve. In a second, the blade was buried deep into the officer's throat.

A gurgled shout from their boss made the recruits turn. In a flash, the one recruit drew and fired wildly with his pistol. The boy was hit, and so was his mother and one of the men. Darren charged in, lifting a geradite rod on the way and then driving it into the gunman's torso, just underneath the armpit. It didn't kill immediately. Darren was caught staring into the eyes of the killer. It was a young man, brown hair with blue eyes. Fearful eyes, blind with tears. Darren didn't know why he did it. Well, sure he did. You didn't let murderers get away with that. You stopped them. You stopped them from killing again – but only by becoming a murderer. You killed to stop the killing, to be killed to stop the killing.

Two other Zonian men had come in and had tackled the other recruit to the floor. They had torn off his mask to reveal another youthful face, filled with fear. The two men pummelled it into the ground, until only a bloody puddle of mush was left.

'Get on the ground!'

Darren turned to see a Yellow with a rifle pointed right at him. Darren knew he was shaking. His laser sight was ducking and diving all over Darren's chest. Under his darkened visor, Darren knew that the Yellow's face was slick with sweat and as white as void. He didn't want to kill Darren. He didn't want to kill, even to stop the killing. He wasn't a killer. He was a bully's lackey.

Darren put his hands up and slowly lowered himself to the floor. As he did so, he lowered his hands. The nervous Yellow didn't notice. As fast as its previous owner, Darren grabbed the pistol and fired a single shot into the Yellows head.

When you mean to stop the killing, you need to be willing to kill. The cycle cannot be stopped. Only renewed. Zonians were the pinnacle of this cycle. They kept on killing. Killing each other. Killing others. Kill, kill, kill.

Those around him just stared, at him, the Yellows and the dead mother and son.

Darren ejected the cartridge from the pistol and counted the rounds – eight left. He inserted the cartridge back into the pistol and checked the chamber. Bullet in the chamber. Nine shots. Kill, kill, kill.

'What you waiting for, lads?'

That seemed to wake them up. Screams were echoing from around the camp. The smell of gunpowder and plasma invaded their nostrils. They had been pushed around long enough. What Dedelux and his Yellows didn't understand is that Zonians were rodents. They would push his people into the corner, forgetting that the cornered zot would bite the cat.

'I've had a vokken 'nuff of living like a pitslug!'

'Yeah!' the group shouted in unison.

'Let's go make those Yellows wear real Trooper colours.'

Darren had not been a fighter on Zona Nox. He'd been a store owner, the victim of the criminal enterprise, but he knew how to conduct violence. Zona Nox had been free not because it was peaceful, far from it. It was free because it was willing to use violence against violence. Its people had the will to be free. If freedom meant blood, so be it.

A Zonian picked up the rifle and joined Darren's posse. Those unarmed had looted the Yellows of extra guns and batons. Armed, they approached the fires.

Lined up around the entrance to the hangar was a wall of black and yellow. Shields protecting the main body of the force as they closed in on the Zonians. Tear gas flew and shock lances were used to keep the protesters back. Multiple formations were closing in on the Zonians from multiple sides. Many Zonians of varied ages and genders screamed their defiance, but behind them were cowering children, the wounded and the elderly. The defiant were defending their weak while the Yellows herded them. Darren's eyes widened. That was the point. The eviction squads were only meant to get the Zonians out in the open. From there, they were to be rounded up and shot. Dedelux was finally exterminating the scum.

'Dixie,' Darren indicated to the rifleman, 'use that peashooter and make a hole in that wall. Rest of you, get ready to take advantage. Let's bloody them up.'

Troopers in Galis had never tried to stop a riot. There weren't ever any riots in Galis to begin with. People weren't entitled on Zona Nox. You worked, you got fed. Nobody was stopping anyone from working, not in Galis at least. Here, things were different. Zonians didn't know how to riot, but they did know one thing. They knew how to kill.

Killing is real simple. All you had to do was put something where it wasn't supposed to be. A fist in a face. A bullet in a brain. A shiv in the gut. Zonians were a simple people and thus could elevate a simple thing, killing, to an art form.

Dixie lined up the shot and fired.

A shield-bearer fell and the wall broke. Rioters trampled over the terrified Yellows. Every fallen Yellow meant a better armed Zonian as shield, baton, lance and gun were turned on their owners. The Yellow snipers, previously hidden behind the shield-wall and waiting for the Zonians to have their back against the wall, were surprised when men and women found them and tore them apart.

This was the Zonian way. It was brutal. Red Sand, their desert, was the colour of their philosophy. Nothing was won without blood, sweat, or both. When you lived on the frontier, with Xank, Sylith and pirates at your doorstep, you learnt to become acquainted with blood.

A young woman had torn the helmet from a Yellow and was smashing his head in with it. Her face was covered with blood and rage. Darren knew her and knew that the corpse lying beside her was her sister. He now knew why he killed. Why they all killed and had been killing their entire lives. You push anyone too far, and they'll crack.

Zonians had bled their entire life. On Nova Zarxa, they bled every day without anything to show for it. It was time they made someone else bleed. And they did. For every one of their dead, they killed ten times that amount. There were no half measures for a Zonian. You killed or you died.

They had cleared the hangar and were pushing out. Yellow reinforcements retreated at their approach, finally locking them into the tower. The Zonians didn't waste time banging on the door. They barricaded it themselves and set a guard. They counted the weapons and tended the wounded.

There was no rejoicing but a sense of relief was felt among all the sons and daughters of Zona Nox. They were no longer slaves to the whims of Dedelux. They threw off their shackles.

They were free.

"Countless news networks exist within human space. Many of these have differing opinions, agendas and topics. The Trooper networks report on security matters, Aegis deals with technology while every planet has their own (if not multiple) main global news outlets. But with all this news, people still find it almost impossible to find the truth." – Lorenzo Gerola, Journalist

Chapter 13. <u>Governor</u>

It had become easy to gain an audience with Dedelux after Marshal gave his identity. There were many fans of his accomplishments, even here on Nova Zarxa. Ganymede was a distant, but still vivid memory for many. Even after the Grag-Tec letter of admission given by Quok had failed, Marshal won them entry.

'What do you think he'll say,' James asked of Marshal.

'I don't know for certain. I don't like him but I don't need to for him to give the order to prepare defences. We need him to call to Mars for aid. Winston will send the host if he does so.'

Marshal looked concerned. He had every right to be with an Imperial invasion on the way, but James sensed that there were other reasons for his mood.

The double-doors to Dedelux's office were ostentatious. Heavily varnished red wood made up most of the surface, with gold inlaid into gaudy patterns along the edges. A mural of Dedelux himself stood central in the doorway.

Marshal pushed both doors inward as he entered the office. Dedelux looked up from his desk, a look of surprise and irritation on his face.

'What is the meaning of this?'

'We come with dire news,' James said, making his way in front of Marshal. 'An Imperial fleet is on the way to Nova Zarxa.'

Surprising Marshal and James, Dedelux laughed at this. It was a sick laugh, filled with contempt.

'What proof do you have of this outrageous claim – Troopers, I presume?'

James threw the documents that Aven had given onto Dedelux's desk. He explained as Dedelux paged through them.

'Grag-Tec ships picked up that information just a few sectors away. They're closing in.'

Dedelux stared down at the pages again and then discarded them into a bin by the side of his desk.

'What...' James started but was interrupted.

'I am not a fan of soldiers taking on missions that I have not assigned to them. I have made it abundantly clear that this is my planet and, therefore, I am in charge.'

'Sir, I was not acting insubordinately. I was delivering information given by my chartered employers at Grag-Tec.'

'Maybe it is high time those corporations lose their protection,' Dedelux whispered under his breath. James was only able to hear it due to his Tetsushisen abilities.

'I will not have my command influenced by corporate mercenaries! These documents are negligible.'

Marshal piped in with all the fury of a gunship. 'You aren't talking to any two chartered Troopers, Governor! You're talking to two battle-forged Veterans. The Troopers are built on experience – how many trenches have you lain in? How many times have you pulled the trigger? Those documents are proof that YOU need to call for aid from

Mars. We can't afford to lose this rock. You have the power to save your so-called planet. If you like your position so much, then listen to reason!'

Dedelux's shock wore off quickly and he responded with fire. 'Who are you to shout at the sovereign Governor of this here city?'

Marshal interrupted him.

'I'm the damn Marshal Rekkie of Zona Nox, slayer of Ganymede, survivor of the Terra excursion and owner of a Terra-damn tank! I'm higher ranked than you, meaning I don't have to listen to your mozar-skite! You are going to investigate those reports properly and then you will see that you have no choice but to call for aid!'

A heavy silence fell over the room as Marshal stared Dedelux square in the eyes. Two personalities were at odds and James, Warpmancer or not, did not want to risk harm by intervening.

Dedelux finally inhaled and then exhaled. He closed his eyes calmly and then spoke without raising his voice.

'Guards!'

Yellow arm-banded Troopers rushed into the room to restrain a stunned Marshal and James.

'You're dooming us all!' Marshal yelled, as he was dragged by three brute Troopers.

'Your charter days are over, Troopers,' Dedelux said as he stood to see them out. 'I hereby pronounce you, with my authority as Planetary Governor, guilty of treason. You are both dishonourably discharged.'

Marshal kicked and fought against the guards but James reserved his strength. He looked calm but that was far from the truth. He was writhing in anger – cold hot rage.

Dedelux was an Imperial agent. There was no other reason for his blatant disregard for both Trooper tenets and the evidence they had shown him. He now knew that someone was onto his lords. They would be ready.

James would have to be faster, smarter and stronger than he had ever been before. He could no longer rely on the power of others to reach his goals. He needed his own power. His own command. His own army.

James knew that it was time for him to become a god. Defiantly, he allowed the guards to drag him to the icy metal cells of Nexus' prison.

❖

Nathan was in the mess hall, as he always was, when he heard news of Marshal and James' capture. A non-Yellow Zarxian sergeant named Yobu had been spreading the news around the mess hall during his guard duty. With so few Troopers left to be shipped out, they had only assigned one guard. When Nathan spoke to him, he said that he'd been in James' squad on Zona Nox.

'He was a great leader. An almost inhuman fighter. He was willing to do whatever it took to get us to safety.'

Nathan explained to him how he knew James. Yobu was in awe. A group of Troopers were now surrounding them.

'James…captured?'

'Marshal, the slayer…couldn't be.'

'Yes,' Yobu repeated, 'James and Marshal were arrested at midday. Dedelux has dishonourably discharged them for treason.'

'Marshal is a legend!' a young Trooper piped in, 'He's more loyal to Mars than Dedelux could ever be.'

The group nodded.

'What does this mean for us?' Nathan asked Yobu.

Yobu shook his head. 'Nothing good. You are the last shipment out of here. By tomorrow, there will be no Zona Nox Trooper left on Nova Zarxa, except for James and Marshal.'

'And Frank! We can't leave them,' a burly Trooper named Ruble exclaimed.

The group in its entirety voiced their agreement, all except Nathan.

'What is it, Nathan?' Ruble questioned.

'We can't simply stay here. They'd gun us down.'

'There is a way,' Yobu whispered. The entire group hushed and moved in to listen.

'This building is currently running on skeleton staff. Dedelux has been moving most of us out of Nexus. Most Troopers still in Nexus are being used for crowd control. The Zona Nox refugees have been rioting and shooting them has only made them angrier. We could all break out of here and go into hiding in one of the outskirt mines, from there we can plan to break out Marshal and James.

'Any danger?' Nathan asked.

'There's always danger but I don't see what choice we have. Let's go. Now!'

There wasn't any further discussion. They collected their belongings and with only one gun among all of them, broke out of Dedelux's house arrest. In the eyes of the law, they were no longer Troopers.

"The arms of the law are long - but most often, not long enough." – Former Sheriff Glint of Red City

Chapter 14. <u>Mutagen</u>

Searchlights, drone patrols, automated turrets…Leri was getting tired of the lack of challenge.

His Bexong Rebels were not a seasoned or trained fighting force but their attacks on the Xank showed the extent of their frustration. No metallic shell could defend the Xank drones against Leri's people. With spear, talon and beak, they broke the armour of their oppressors. There had been deaths, but that was to be expected. Only Gura-Teng showed gloom at the loss of his comrades. Everyone else was too busy moving forward, slaying their enemies. Revolution did not stop to mourn.

Leri, Rii as they called him, crouched low on the brink of a cliff-face overlooking a large metal structure. The building was a shining black cube. It had no windows and no entrances. It seemed impenetrable. Leri knew better. Peron had sent him all information that he needed on how to assault these facilities. The design itself was based purely on keeping enemies out. It was a prison, but its inhabitants were more mentally enslaved than physically.

Regardless, the future of his people depended upon its destruction. The gargantuan cube was a breeding facility and Leri knew that the male Zangorians had been too long without family. The same went for the females.

As night fell, they made their way down the slopes of the surrounding cliff faces. The cube had been shot down from orbit by the Xank all those decades ago and the act had left a massive crater. Xank engineers had found themselves regretting this means of construction as the craters had the habit of being filled with water. Drainage pipes had been installed, but the costs had surpassed the alternative means of construction.

They had been watching the floating drone patrols for hours and had a decent idea of their patterns. They determined an opening and went for it. In a storm of sand, covered by darkness, a group of ten Zangorians found themselves alongside Leri at the base of the cube. None of them spoke and only the slight thump of their footfalls betrayed their presence.

If Leri's memory served him right, this was the right place. He took a device out of his satchel and placed it upon the wall. He stomped his foot twice to signal his comrades. After three seconds, there was a pop and a sizzle. Leri and another Zangorian took their position in the dark and clutched the edges of the now cut-out piece of metal.

The plasma-cutter had done its job, as Peron had promised. One by one, Leri and his rebels entered the facility.

The halls were bright. Piercing white walls and tiles hurt Leri's night-tuned eyes. The passages reminded Leri of the bunkers beneath Fort Nox. White was not a normal colour to be used by the Xank, and now that Leri thought about it, not by the Human Troopers. The reason for its use was that it was exceptionally easy to spot enemies within it. The orange feathers of a Zangorian would stand out like an oasis in the desert.

Leri was not afraid of the drones within the facility – only the turrets surrounding it. Now that they were bypassed, he had no qualms fighting the drones within. As much as it benefitted him, Leri couldn't help but find the drones shameful. They were almost useless in a fight and relied on fear and indoctrination for their power. Leri's fighters slew them easily. Yet, Leri had never ventured into a facility such as this. He did not know what the Xank had in case of breaches. There may or may not be something far greater than puny drones in these metal halls. Regardless, they had to press on. Kuru-spear and tiao-swords at the ready.

Behind them, two Zangorians lifted the circular metal sheet that had fallen as a result of the plasma-cutter and placed it back in the hole. The sheet melded back into the wall as if it hadn't fallen at all. Only the trained eye could see the seams. They had used the device many times before. Peron had gifted an armoury of them to get Leri's forces used to the idea of stealthy sabotage. It was working and the Bexong Rebels had successfully used the Word Lectorate technology to enter many enemy facilities, unbeknownst to the Xank.

Ten-pa, a young Bexong Zangorian, signed to Leri that their point of entry was now hidden. Leri nodded. Ten-pa was a studious and devoted young-one. His feathers were still a light orange and his beak had yet to accumulate the growths of age. Despite this, his tenacity and loyalty soon saw him rise to Leri's second-in-command.

They advanced further into the facility.

There were no signs or any means of finding direction, so Leri chose paths randomly.

'There is only one target in the breeding cube – the Main Console. Everything can be shut down from that machine,' Leri recalled his orders from Peron.

They turned through a doorway, where Leri stopped. Lines and lines of pods filled a titanic hall. The room was black with every pod emanating a sullen blue.

Leri approached a pod and gazed at its contents.

'Rii...' one of the rebels, Xupa squeaked. Leri did not chastise him for speaking. He was also shocked enough to break protocol.

In the pod was a child.

Its beak was small and its feathers yet to grow fully. It looked like something out of a horror – a malformed mutant. Leri knew better. This was how the Xank altered their Zangorians to fulfil their purpose. To the Xank, every Zangorian was a tool. They were used as cannon fodder, lab experiments, breeders and slaves. Xank generals referred to them as the Body Budget.

Leri smashed his metal fist into the pod, smashing the glass. Released of its genetically modifying ooze, the child Zangorian withered and died. The Bexong rebels stared, aghast.

'You killed it,' Xupa whispered.

'There was nothing left to kill.'

Leri stared down the long stretch of coffins. There was nothing in here to save.

It was hours later when they reached their first closed door. The steel door was round and seemed to roll open and closed, with clamps to keep it in place.

There were no buttons or keypads, so Leri presumed that the gate was opened remotely, most probably by an organic official. There was no way that they were waiting for an Immortal to appear on one of his annual rounds. They had to get in now.

'Do we have any more plasma cutters?' Leri signed.

'No,' was the reply from Yuy.

Leri made his way to the door and tapped. They weren't getting in without plasma.

At that moment, triggered by the sound of metal on metal, an automated turret descended from a tile on the roof and fired a gush of blue energy at Yuy. The plasma disintegrated the Zangorian's chest in one hit.

Everyone dove for cover but Leri. As the turret swivelled, firing at the panicking Zangorians, Leri threw his kuru. The spear glanced off the turret, but Leri wasn't hoping for any damage. What he was counting on was threat classification. The turret swivelled 360 degrees and aimed at him. He was the threat.

Leri stood completely still.

'Rii!' Xupa shouted, as a blast of energy was released from the turret.

At the last moment, Leri dodged out of the way, allowing the blast to penetrate the steel door, revealing a hole the size of a fist. Leri waited for another blast and dodged again. A bigger hole. He kept doing this until the hole was big enough to climb through, then he sprinted towards the turret and jumped. His metal talon dug into the weak artificial alloy. Leri found it pitifully easy to crush the machine.

Threat averted, the group approached Yuy.

'We'll give him a proper funeral,' Ten-pa avowed, closing Yuy's terrified eyes with his knuckles.

'Gura-teng will be saddened. Another death,' Tepri added.

'Some must die for all to be free,' Leri announced, with a tone of finality.

Everyone nodded. Leri led the way through the hole. This room was dark and dusty. It was seldom used and with good reason. From here, the facility was shut down. It was a small room, gloomy. A single screen in a large boxy machine was the only source of light.

'When you come to the Main Console,' Peron had said, 'you'll know the password.'

Leri was dubious but didn't question the Gleran.

With his Bexong Rebels watching him, Leri advanced towards the terminal.

Upon its white screen was a single black symbol. It was a scratchy symbol of a forgotten language. Gone…not forgotten, Leri corrected himself. He remembered, even though he was not there. It was his past self who remembered.

The Xank used to let Zangorians man and guard the facilities. It was only five decades ago that they introduced drone guards. Leri – no - Leri's ancestor was one of the last Zangorian guards here. He had been put to death, as he too knew the truth of Zeruit. He had shut down the facility with the console he had made, ensuring that it was so entrenched into the facility that removing it would destroy everything.

Leri saw an entire life in the span of a second. This was not like the garbled memories he had once mistaken as his own. This was an observation of an existence. Like a voyeur, Leri saw his ancestor born, live and die. Right down to the final crushing of his ancestor's head by an Immortal, Leri remembered.

He saluted a life lived and a sacrifice made. He knew that the password could not be changed. His ancestor had started this plot fifty years ago. He knew that someone of his seed would finally reach this point.

Leri tapped the screen to reveal an onscreen keyboard. He wrote the password: Kazh-aira.

It was accepted and at once, the facility shut down. The distant hum of drones and electricity stopped and all the lights went off at once.

Kazh-aira had ended this atrocity. Leri was disappointed to find that this was not a breeding ground where he could save females, but rather a mutation centre, but he felt relief at ending the suffering of these impure Zangorians.

With his ancestor's memory, he didn't only find the password, however. He also found his next target. Kazhaira was their new goal, and they would save their women.

"Zonian nationalism was fundamentally caused by the persecution of refugees by Dedelux. Through an attempt to destroy potential enemies and 'drags on the state', Dedelux created his ultimate destruction." – M. Robble, Human Historian

Chapter 15. <u>Fought the Law</u>

Dedelux's prison tower rose like a monolith from the glowing fields below. Icy geradite created a cold, blue exterior, with a single doorway, through which Marshal, James and a group of convicts were now being marched.

There had never been a prison on Zona Nox. There were jails, sure. Marshals and sheriffs would confine the convicted until justice was done. But prisons were a different story. An entire building dedicated to the housing of wrongdoers – no – those perceived wrongdoers. It was an unnecessary extravagance. Prisons were an odd thing, James thought. In Galis, you had courts. They were community courts, or linked to the gangs or corporations. The Troopers even had a court. They were there to administer the confusing matters of justice. For the simpler, stabby and shooty kind of justice, lynch mobs tended to know better than any uppity Trooper trying to make Galis into a new Mars. Zona Nox justice wasn't perfect, James knew that, but prisons just didn't make sense to him. Why commit to holding criminals when you could use the very same resources to stop them completely? Maybe James was just less remorseful. Ironic, seeing that he would be the one under the guillotine.

Marshal and James were marched from the icy prison entrance down a long geradite hallway. Through force gates and barred doors, they passed offices, cells, guards and syns. With Marshal and James was a group of around eight convicts. All of them wore bright orange jumpsuits and coded hand-restraints. Only the mag-keys of the wardens could open the restraints.

The guards were better-equipped than the average Yellow in the city. They were armoured from head to toe, carrying shotguns, hand-guns and shock-batons. James suspected that even better equipped assault Troopers resided behind some of the closed doors, in case of a riot.

They stopped in a hall lined on either side by cells, barricaded with geradite bars. Each cell contained three to four orange clad inmates, sitting forlornly around electric heaters. Almost none of the inmates looked like threats. They were puny, with no muscles or even facial hair. It was evident that these were not violent criminals – if criminals at all. James had heard that violence was prevalent in prisons, and thus genders were separated to prevent sexual assault – but these cells were mixed. Both women and men resided in these cells, staring hopelessly into the white lights of the heaters.

A shout from the warden got them moving again. The guards, it seemed, were putting on increased armour and arming themselves with shock lances. They moved down the hallway. Only a few of the convicts looked up at them.

The door at the end of the hallway was triple-guarded. A gate let one enter into a holding chamber that then revealed a blast door and then a force gate. James was almost flattered that they would undergo so much effort to keep him in check.

The crescent-shaped room aligned the entire half of the prison tower. Cells guarded by force gates lined the walls like a hive. Those contained in the cells James could peer into looked like real threats. Tattooed, muscular, scarred and hard-faced. The women in the cells made the men in the other hall look like sexless children. This was where the

Trooper dissidents had been hidden. Behind bars, blast door and force gate were those Troopers who had defied Dedelux – or had known too much. It seemed that for one reason or another, the Yellows needed them alive.

As they marched down spiral floors and besides force-cells, James recognised many Trooper faces. Frank McGraff was there, nodding to James with respect.

Whistle-blowers, dissidents, disobedient Troopers. This was the high security section of Dedelux's personal prison. The place where he made his enemies disappear to maintain his superficial façade of success. This was going to be James' home – even if only for a while. James didn't know how he would get out, but he knew he would. Krag-Zot wouldn't let the humans confine his god for long, and if not that, Aven was sure to release him through some odd contacts.

James saw the reason why the Yellows had armed themselves with the long shock-lances as they stopped by a cell with one inmate in it. The resident – a burly mountain of a man – immediately charged the Yellows, just to receive a zap that knocked him back. If the Yellows had to rely on batons, the long arms of the assailant would have reached their jaws first.

One of the convicts with the group was shoved into the cell. Then they moved on. Convicts in ones and twos were dropped off in cells with room. Until there was only James and Marshal. They were led down a long hallway until they reached a fork. They split and Marshal was led away from James.

Ushered along, James was finally shown to his new home. It was a dark, cold cell, with nothing but a toilet and hard-looking pallet.

'Be defiant as you want now, "Trooper",' one of the guards gloated, shoving him in with the butt of his lance and then shutting the force gate behind him.

James didn't utter a word.

❖

It was never cold in Nexus. Nova Zarxa was always cold, but Baryu Targa had never felt cold before. The lights and heaters were always kept on in the Nexus central towers. The Governor made sure that his people were always warm, always well-lit and always entertained. Baryu had been in the process of such entertainment, watching a recording of an Astro-Race, when the screen switched off and the lights started to flicker.

Then the heat fell.

This is mighty peculiar, he thought. Nothing like this had ever happened before. Could screenies even be turned off? When were lights ever off in Nexus? When were they ever flickering? Baryu had lived in Nexus all fifty-three years of his life and none of this had ever happened before.

Immediately, he lurched from his armchair and left his two-room apartment. His apartment was located above a screen-repair shop, along a balcony connecting several other apartments which were above even more shops. Each shop was lit well with neon lighting, which was not flickering. Some of Baryu's neighbours had left their apartments as well.

'Screen off, Jenny?' Baryu asked a pink-haired lady holding a small domesticated vowl.

'Yeah, and right through my shows! What's going on?'

'Nothing good. Can't be good if it has never happened before.'

It looked as if Jenny was about to say something when the ground shook. Jenny dropped the vowl which then proceeded to run around her legs, yapping away and chewing at the edge of her gown.

Police were rushing down the hall, holding scary guns. Baryu didn't like guns, but he wasn't afraid of the police. They were there to help.

The ground shook again. This time they heard a bang and some hisses. A voice on an intercom sounded.

'Please evacuate this sector. There has been a critical malfunction. Please evacuate this sector.'

The announcement repeated itself, alongside a rather unpleasant siren.

'Agh, going to miss the next round.'

Baryu had been looking forward to watching the race between Pluto and Titan live.

The residents of the complex calmly began walking down the stairs and towards the exit. Then there was a deafening roar and smoke. A flash, a bang and then a whooshing suction.

Baryu opened his eyes as he felt the cold bite at him. He had never felt it before. He had never smelt the cold, noxious air of his home. It didn't smell like the crisp, minty smell of geradite but of rotting meat that Baryu had encountered once in the lower sectors. As he began to smell the fumes, he collapsed. He coughed and coughed. He doubled over and after hurling, saw that his bile was red.

All he wanted was to watch Pluto beat Titan. They were looking very good this season. Then there was black.

❖

Groups of inmates could watch screens at certain intervals throughout the day. They made sure that inmates who knew each other well never coincided but that didn't stop James from getting acquainted with some strangers.

The mountain of a man from before was named Alex Yurgan. He was from Titan and used to be a spacecraft mechanic at a docking station. He joined up with Obsidian when the pay was good and had moved to Nova Zarxa when Obsidian was expanding into Extos III. Later, downscaling left him destitute. He decided to do work for Dedelux but after he got perturbed that his pay wasn't getting in on time, he lodged a complaint and ended up here. In Nexus, you could live a cushy life – if you never complain and never showed any sign of criticising the regime.

It was quite incongruent that such a violent looking man had been arrested for such a petty offence. He stated that the only reason he was in the maximum-security section was because he had made a game of scaring the guards. He had become immune to shock lance jolts years ago, and was only putting on an act of submission so to avoid worse security measures. James doubted that the man was even immune to the shocks. A crater in his arm revealed where the man had ripped out a Dedelux monitoring device from his flesh. Rather than be immune, James rather guessed that Alex Yurgan couldn't feel pain.

James and Yurgan spent much of their time in the mess hall, watching screens and talking. James had told Yurgan about his escapades and arrest – blotting out the sensitive details. Yurgan was impressed.

This day, there was no talking. Everyone's faces were aimed at the screen. A newscaster in the pay of Dedelux's regime was reporting on violence in one of the central residence towers. A bridge had been bombed by a projectile coming from an unknown source. Fifty Nexus citizens had died. Dedelux appeared on the screen:

'Citizens of Nexus, my friends and family. This is a grave and tragic day which has brought us to mourn the loss of our countrymen. Terrorists have attacked our people! They are jealous of our prosperity and wish to sink our city into chaos. Stay strong, Zarxians. We will not let these terrorists and their collaborators get away with this. They will be brought to justice and your safety and warmth will once again be assured.

'The Nexus Civil Police Corps have assured me that everything will be under control shortly. In the meanwhile, we will need to tolerate some restrictive procedures. Curfews will now be in effect. Please refer to your wrist-tab for notices. Bridges will also now be under control by NCPC. To accommodate this change, private enterprise will be put under control of the state. Grag-Tec has been found to be collaborating with the Zonian terrorists and will now be treated as a criminal entity. Please report any sightings of known Grag-Tec officials and employees to NCPC. Rewards will be provided.

'Once again, citizens, these are dark times. But Nova Zarxa is a dark planet and Nexus is a shining beacon in this void of evil. Strength and unity. Hail Nexus!'

The news report ended and the programme was changed to the news that Titan beat Pluto in the Astro-races, a fact that would result in many suicides by doting fans of the defending champions.

'Seems your people are a lot less tolerant of dictators than the usual bunch, eh,' Alex stated, picking his nails with a plastic fork.

'Never knew Zonians to bomb anything. We were more prone to shooting and stabbing. This is odd.'

James was concerned. He could believe that his people, a violent people, would kill Nexus citizens who got in their way, but not wantonly blow up an entire building causing the residents to choke on crystal fumes. That wasn't the Zonian way.

'This isn't Zonian work.'

A few of the inmates turned to him. Alex was interested, but half-watching the Astro-race replays.

'How'd you know?' a Zarxian convict asked. He was booked for smuggling and had killed a Yellow in the process of being arrested.

'When a Zonian wants to kill, they look you in the eyes first. They let you know they're there.'

James stood and walked towards the convict.

'They take the knife out slowly, make sure you hear the flick. They don't hide their colours. They make sure you know which gang they're from – then they gut you.'

The Zarxian was leaning back. He nodded and James nodded back, returning to his seat.

❖

James nimbly dodged to the side as a shock lance flew towards him. Its sparks illuminated his face in blue. He grabbed the staff and pulled its owner towards him. The Yellow Trooper was wide-eyed as James ripped off his mask and punched him straight in the jaw. The man dropped and James used his new weapon to put down another charging guard. Alex Yurgan was also making headway, head-butting a Yellow and beating him with his own baton.

The cafeteria was a mess. Chairs and tables had been erected as barricades. The convicts used the furniture as a laager against the waves of riot control troops.

Few of them believed that this riot would amount to anything, but James and Marshal did not care. It had been made clear to them weeks ago that the guards were not cleared to kill them. Until a point, the guards would have to tolerate most of their actions – even riots.

James had no problem batting a thrown flashbang back into the hall. He even laughed as he did so. This was a game. It was a contest of Zarxian sensibilities versus Zonian brinkmanship. James didn't care who broke first. He knew that he had very little time and not much to lose. Destabilising Dedelux's regime from the prison was all he could accomplish at present. It would have to do.

A convict cried out as a projectile hit him in the stomach. James took cover as rubber balls pelted the tables at high speed. These were fake guns. They did not kill honestly. They wounded and hurt, so that the enemy would give up. Many of the Zarxian convicts did give up. The Zonians did not.

James picked up a dining tray, indicating for others to do the same. A group of them then charged, stolen riot gear and make-shift shields, towards the rubber gunners. The guards broke before they could close the gap, retreating in fear.

After weeks behind electrified bars, James and Marshal, unbeknownst to the other, had reached breaking point. They knew of the tight schedule. Their lives were forfeit if Nova Zarxa was unable to establish a strong enough defence, and that defence would require the end of Dedelux's rule. So, they did the only thing they knew how. They fought. They beat up guards. They incited riots. They committed arson and vandalism so that the prison guards could never relax. After the first riot, they were knocked out and returned to their cells. This had bemused James.

Why not kill us?

After careful experimentation, involving the assault of Dedelux's Yellows, they determined that political prisoners were not allowed to be killed. While curious about the reason for this bizarre policy, James had not hesitated to use it to his advantage.

Over the weeks, he and Marshal would sabotage and riot – doing their part for the Zonian rebellion that they viewed on the screens. They battered the prison guards – never killing, but taking up their time as much as possible.

In this most recent riot, they had held the cafeteria past curfew for around three hours. They had plenty of food to sustain the rebellion and had become practiced in batting away stun grenades and blocking rubber bullets. Eventually, James and his comrades began to tire.

'Okay, chaps. Time to rest. Let's give them a breather,' James ordered.

They laid down their arms and assembled in the middle of the hall, hands on their heads. Yellows poured in, slowly and calmly. They knew that this was not a trick. That was against the rules. They also knew not to harm the prisoners, or restrain them, for that would result in yet another riot – one that could result in death.

Yet, this did not calm James. Killing was natural. In the Yellow's shoes, he would have killed all the convicts after the first riot. There had to be a reason for this unreasonable sense of leniency. A reason that was much darker and terrifying than anything within this colossal prison.

❖

The bandana-masked individual with the stolen Trooper helmet counted down with his fingers, silently being watched by three more individuals.

Three fingers. Two. One.

As he closed his hand in a fist, he tossed a cooked grenade through the doorway. The individual opposite him followed the explosion, opening fire on the occupants of the room with a home-made shotgun.

'Clear!' Dixie announced.

Darren followed Annabelle into the room.

Three had been killed by the grenade. Two more by Dixie. The Zonian rebels fanned out into the storeroom. Annabelle and Jordan had been Zenites back in Galis. They knew how to clear a room. Their insane boss had wanted to build an army to take Galis, after all. They had been trained to be professional. They now used this military precision to clear the room and check it for danger.

'Darren, we have three minutes to take what we need,' Jordan explained.

Darren nodded and got to work. Dixie was put on guard duty, at the doorway. The rest of them filled carry bags with gas tanks, batteries and charge crystals. These resources would keep their people alive for a few more days.

'Time's up.'

They didn't delay their exit. When the Yellows came to investigate the disturbance, they were already long gone.

❖

'What brutes!'

'Savages…'

'Yes, complete barbarians.'

These were the utterances across the main hall of the Peixes do espaço. Erryn Kolheim listened on from her table by the window, glancing occasionally from the menu of

Grengen imported fish. The powdered and plastic people of the hall were very different from her. While they wore the gaudy and neon mono-coloured clothes of the Zarxian rich, she wore her work clothes – a greasy black dark grey tank top and cargo pants. She had been stopped at the door, but a credit check allowed her through.

A ship's pilot may be unkempt, but they were seldom poor.

Erryn Kolheim was a Zarxian by birth – technically. She was born in a ship docked in Nexus. This ship had been her home ever since, as it travelled human space – shipping goods wherever they needed shipping. The Kolheim had stood the test of time for a century and would continue to do so if she had anything to say about it.

'Turn it up, concierge!' one of the patrons ordered. There was no opposition.

Erryn half-listened, half-ordered, as the screen's volume was turned up.

'Zonian terrorists have murdered five civilians in a brutal attack. Trooper officials state that the civilians were murdered in a desperate effort to attack a Trooper ammunition storeroom. No Troopers were killed, as they managed to scare off the terrorists. This comes as the fifth attack this week. No Zonian official has agreed to comment.'

Erryn snorted. *More likely they weren't being allowed to comment.*

'Scum. Murderous scum. Did you know any of them?'

'No, no. But they must have had families. Poor dears.'

Erryn dug into her fish, Grengen carp, as she listened to the screen. She didn't truly care for the details. It was just to pass the time. She seldom spent time on Nova Zarxa. In fact, she was only here to try out the fish that they had recently shipped in. The rebellion of these Zonian refugees was a small affair to her. She had been to Zona Nox once and had not been impressed. Most of its inhabitants had never even gone into space. Bunch of dirt-birthers, as she and her comrades would disparage them. There was very little mutual ground. Neither did their plight mean much to her. There were wars, famines, plagues and refugee crises every day across human space. She witnessed many. This was no different. This rebellion was just growing pains. She was accustomed to Dedelux's repression. She didn't like it, but she knew to keep her head down while planetside. She had space to be free. She felt sorry for the dirt birthing Zonians, but they'd learn. They'd have to. To be honest, she didn't much care. She had her ship. The Kolheim was all she needed to be free. This wasn't a fight she was going to get involved in. She had enough of those dodging Pegg pirates and brigands.

'In light of repeated terrorist attacks, Governor Dedelux has ordered all space vessels to be impounded until further notice. This prohibition on space travel will end once the crisis is over.'

Erryn spat out her cola.

She ran to the screen. Her ears hadn't deceived her. On the screen, a reporter stood in front of the Kolheim, as Yellow Troopers marched its crew outside, clamping it to the docking bay.

Filled with fury, Erryn paid her bill and marched outside of the restaurant. This was now her fight.

❖

James had lost count of the days. They were no longer allowed to meet in the cafeteria. Everyone was confined to their rooms. The last time he had seen a screen, the news was that an entire skyscraper had been taken by the Zonian terrorists. Dedelux had declared martial law to maintain order.

Zonian – it was an odd term. James had never thought of himself as a Zonian. He was a Galisian, at most. Mostly, he had been a Marzio made-man. His identity was in his allegiance, not some arbitrary place of birth. But now Zonians did find identity in a form of allegiance. By attacking them all as one, Dedelux had ensured that the Zonians had become one. Ironic that the Zonian nation had been formed by attempts at its destruction.

But wasn't that always the way? You push too hard, and something pushes back. Yellows shot at Zonians, so Zonians shot back. That was the way of the world.

James only hoped that his people wouldn't go too out of control. His was a violent people. He recognised that. Violence was natural. It was a necessity in a harsh reality – but not the optimum. While James had told the convict that Zonians wouldn't kill civilians, he knew otherwise.

Zonians would kill. There would be reason to the killing, yes, but killing civilians could be justified. But was it worth it? James hoped it never would be.

James was a killer. One of the best killers. But even he wished that he would not have to kill again. As he lay in his cell, he dreamed of such a place but knew that to get there, there would be plenty of killing along the way.

The Zonians would continue killing. Dedelux didn't give them a choice. He was a born tyrant. He was used to subjects, not individuals. Zonians weren't subjects nor citizens. They were individuals. James, as one of them, knew this. Zonians formed groups not to be ruled over, but to work together for their own and each other's benefit. It wasn't by the obedience of the Zonian that things got done, but by the simple fact that things needed doing. This was what made them free. Zonians refused to be dependent. They refused to be slaves.

James, in chains and behind bars, refused to be a slave. He contemplated what Krag-Zot had once told him, that freedom could only be given by the powerful. That wasn't freedom. That was permissive slavery. Freedom wasn't a state of permissiveness – it was independence. In a group or alone, but by choice and not by the whims of a tyrant.

James knew this and so did his people. Zonians were free because they chose to be so. James was free, even behind bars, because he refused to give up. Freedom wasn't given. It was taken from the bloodied hands of tyrants.

Chapter 16. <u>Glossary</u>

Swearwords (in order of severity)

Void – equivalent to hell, a term some humans still use.

Zot (zoot) – a scaly rodent, insult used to refer to the untrustworthy.

Grako – one who has forgotten the face of their father.

Skite – broad meanings. Typically, a waste product or trash, or a sign of severity.

Vok (as written) – broad meanings. Typically, an adjective to describe the intolerable.

Vushla – Imperial swearword. Roughly translates to: From all that is the most vokked up, this is more so.

Races

Edal – blue, pointy-eared humanoid mammals often called the Star Folk. Founding race of the Imperial Council.

Exanoid – pig-like mammals standing on two short legs, with a permanently bow-bent spine. Renowned as traders, scientists and business-people due to their constant transactions with humans.

Gleran – hive-mind insects controlled through pheromones produced by a sentient queen.

Gray – grey-skinned, hermaphrodite mammals, typically found subservient to other races.

Human – a race of mammals who have populated much of the region of space known as Free space. If you are reading this, you are probably human.

Krugar – six-armed, legless reptiles with violent skin, mostly dominated by the Xank Empire.

Pegg – large-headed, small mammals who evolved in low gravity. They excel in zero gravity battles in space as pirates, but are unable to perform with medium to high gravity.

Squogg – almost permanently covered humanoids, who wear embalming suits to prevent their bodies decaying from a genetic plague.

Ulyx – tall, snow-white humanoids that breed through parthenogenesis, where some individuals are born fertile while others are not.

Vacaraptor – short, sentient dinosaur resembling reptiles, from Grengen.

Voroz – grey titans who fight for the Imperial Council.

Zangorian – flightless bird humanoids with orange coats of feathers and sharp talons and beaks. Dominated by the Xank Empire.

Planets/Moons

Earth – the human homeworld, since

Ganymede – the largest moon of Jupiter and one of its largest civilian colonies. The battlefield of the Ganymede Incident.

Grengen – a jungle world and homeworld of the vacaraptors, located in Extos III.

Mars – the largest population of any human world. Capital of the Trooper Order.

Nova Zarxa – a crystal mining world neighbouring Zona Nox in the Extos III system.

Zona Nox – a backwater frontier world in the Extos III system.

Historical Events

Fall of Dead Stone – the first major casualty of the First Xank invasion. Dead Stone was the largest city on the planet, and its destruction caused a refugee crisis that culminated into the creation of Galis City.

The Ganymede Incident – the latest Imperial aggression against humanity, where the Imperials occupied the human moon of Ganymede for unknown reason. Many humans and their allies fought to dislodge the invaders.

Glotos III uprising – a grey led rebellion against the exanoid dictator Gwok, which resulted in the founding of the Grag-Tec corporation, in honour of Grag-Po, the rebel's leader.

The Discovery – the Trooper discovery of the descendants of the Zonian crash landers who had been isolated from humanity for over 100 years.

Prominent Factions

Empire of Xank - empire formed of multiple races found in the Outer Reach, beyond the Central Space frontier.

Imperial Council – a mysterious, totalitarian alien empire, and likely the largest empire in the Milky way galaxy.

Trooper Order - human military order founded on Mars which is devoted to the protection and expansion of human owned space. They are pledged to protect humanity across the galaxy.

United Exanoid Federation – a coalition of consenting exanoid dominated corporations, banding together for mutual defence.

Megacorporations

Aegis Corporation (Ee-jis) – human corporation founded on Mars as a shipping company and has since grown to become the largest supplier of high-end computers and combat utilities in human space.

Grag-Tec – a corporation founded jointly by grays and exanoids after the Glotos III uprising. Specialises in robotics and computers.

Obsidian Corporation – a human and exanoid corporation specialising in vehicle development and manufacturing.

Titan Corporation – one of the oldest human megacorporations still in operation. Specialises in armaments, heavy machinery and mining.

Zerian Corporation - a human corporation specialising in cheap commodities and questionable industries.

Terms

Tabs – the shortening of the word tablet. Refers to any small, portable computer. Can range from as large as a contemporary laptop to nanoscopic proportions.

Warp – a mysterious element that can be used to produce energy and facilitate faster-than-light travel.

Terra – the focus of a human-dominated religion. Terra is a metaphor for the spirit of humanity.

Void – a reference to space, death, or just an expletive.

Extos Strip – the three neighbouring systems of Extos I to III.

Overseer – a corporate assigned manager of a frontier venture.

Core Worlds – the high developed worlds of any particular race.

Credits/Creds – money.

Reaper – gigantic mechanised walking vehicles armed with extensive weaponry.

Animals

Sylith – a hive-mind controlled race of giant insects with varying sub-species. They are categorised by their strong exoskeletons and large blade-like appendages.

Vowl – a race of canine scavengers, distantly related to coyotes.

Zot – a catch-all term for any small vermin, typically rats.

Mozar – large, six-legged cattle bred throughout the frontier.

Pecker/Avisulan – flightless, two-legged birds.

Pit-slug – waste eating slugs common in the Galis City canals.

Dating System

Use of the Gregorian calendar is still prevalent but was renamed to the Terran Calendar (TC) at the start of the Armageddon Calendar (AC) which began in the year 2250 TC. Other dating systems used by humans are the Age of the Cape (ACP, 2300 TC) and After Blight (3000 TC).

Trooper Ranks (Highest rank to lowest)

- **High Protector:** First among equals of the Council-Generals. Makes final decision when consensus cannot be achieved. Can be seen as the ruler of the Trooper Order.
- **Council-General:** An almost peerless general tasked with directing the grand strategy of the Order, including the affairs of the Armada, Logistics and Order.
- **Planetary General:** The highest ranking general and commanding officer on a planet.
- **General:** Leads an army made up of 2-5 sections.
- **Force Commander:** Leads a force of 2-5 divisions.
- **Colonel:** Leads a division of 2-5 companies.
- **Captain:** Leads a company of 3-5 platoons.
- **Lieutenant:** Leads a platoon of 3-5 squads.
- **Strike Leader:** Leads a strike team of 10-20 men. Answers to superior officers but not formally a part of any greater structure. Acts semi-independently.
- **Sergeant:** Leads a squad of 6-12 men.
- **Corporal:** Leads a fireteam or section of 2-6 men.
- **Lance Corporal:** Leads a patrol of 1-3 men.
- **Specialist/Corporal:** Specially trained personnel.
- **Private:** Inducted Trooper.
- **Trainee/Recruit:** Informally inducted Trooper.

Notes on Human Language

Unexpectedly, human language has not changed as much in the last one and a half thousand years than one would expect. Proliferation of media and technology in languages led more to a blending of language than any sort of replacement by new dialects.

When humans first encountered aliens, to facilitate easy communication – Standard Terran was developed. The language was mostly the future dialect of English, combined with Portuguese, German-Dutch, Gaelic, Korean and Afrikaans.

Many human worlds speak their own languages, but Standard Terran is the *lingua franca* of the Core Worlds.

Zonian has similar roots to Standard Terran. The original crash-landers were mostly of Scottish origin, blending with a few Cape Federation settlers and some German-Dutchmen.

Due to the vast population of humans in Free Space, most Free Race aliens choose to speak Standard Terran.

Tenets of the Trooper Order

The tenets are by no means a legal document. They were constructed by early Trooper officers to instil a set of values in new recruits.

  I. Fight the enemies of mankind.
  II. Slay the traitors of our race.
  III. Protect humankind.

IV. Prepare to live and die for the Order.
V. Never slay or harm a fellow Trooper.
VI. Relish peace, prepare for war.
VII. Bullets take lives. Skill saves them.
VIII. Pursue the art of our enemies to wreak vengeance upon them.
IX. Blood and Blight, never forget.